NIGHTS OF TERROR

Table of Contents

STEVE FRAZEE
NIGHTS OF TERROR

Edited by Eric Frazee

LEISURE BOOKS NEW YORK CITY

A LEISURE BOOK®

May 2004

Published by special arrangement with Golden West Literary Agency.

Dorchester Publishing Co., Inc.
200 Madison Avenue
New York, NY 10016

ISBN 0-8439-5345-4

The name "Leisure Books" and the stylized "L" with design are trademarks of Dorchester Publishing Co., Inc.

Printed in the United States of America.

Visit us on the web at www.dorchesterpub.com.

NIGHTS OF TERROR

STEVE FRAZEE

NIGHTS OF TERROR

Edited by Eric Frazee

LEISURE BOOKS NEW YORK CITY

A LEISURE BOOK®

May 2004

Published by special arrangement with Golden West Literary Agency.

Dorchester Publishing Co., Inc.
200 Madison Avenue
New York, NY 10016

ISBN 0-8439-5345-4

Visit us on the web at www.dorchesterpub.com.

Foreword

This collection of eight Steve Frazee short stories showcases his ability to cover many different themes while maintaining his own individual style of writing. From comedy to grim reality and all points between, Steve captures the past, as always, with impeccable historical accuracy and a deep understanding of the human psyche. Often the line between hero and villain is clouded. Steve's characters are by no means perfect, and it is that imperfection, coupled with the daily temptations we all experience that adds realism to all his work, regardless of the theme. I hope you enjoy this compilation as much as I did putting it together.

Eric Frazee
Bailey, Colorado

Saddle Sore Gun
from Texas

From the top of Gypsum Hill, Hallidane was just a smear at the end of rails that had come from somewhere out of the Texas vastness. Behind his rock, Brett Meredith watched the stage starting up the grade and thought that soon the bigness of the country was going to be mighty handy.

They wouldn't be expecting trouble just a half mile from town, maybe. Not the driver at least, but little Clyde Betters, riding shotgun today, not only expected but pined for trouble every time he went up on the seat.

The business with Betters would have to be timed to the split second. There was plenty of room to bury a man in this country.

The horses were working hard against the grade, the driver was telling a big lie about the women he'd known in El Paso, and Betters seemed to be drowsing when Meredith sprang from cover and yelled: "Reach, boys!"

The driver locked his wheels, clamped the lines between his knees, and reached. Still appearing half asleep, Betters flicked his shotgun in line and shot without raising it.

Meredith's timing was right as he dived for cover, but he had no protection against the piece of buck that slammed off a rock and buried itself in the fleshy part of his thigh.

Betters's second barrel took the crown off Meredith's hat as he ducked. It was a flat-crowned hat with a chin thong. He jerked it back in place on his thick thatch of rusty-red hair.

From the rocks on the other side of the stage, Jack Sarrett stepped out and called: "Never mine reloading, Betters! And just leave the carbine where it is."

With one hand halfway to a carbine in the boot, Betters straightened slowly, his thin face bitter. "That was the dirtiest trick that was ever pulled on me," he said.

Sarrett laughed. "Next time we'll show you a really good one. Live and learn, Betters." He said to Meredith: "Get busy while the boys are coming down to stretch their legs. No passengers today."

The leather-covered box under the driver's boards wasn't heavy. *It will be easy to carry,* Meredith thought happily. Sarrett had been right again. But you couldn't trust these Wells Fargo people too far. He smashed the lock and seal with Betters's carbine.

They hadn't been fooling. The contents were crisp and green.

"Got a new partner now, eh, Sarrett?" Betters said.

"You mean Bill? Oh, sure. . . ."

"Bill, hell!" the driver said.

Sarrett laughed so easily and with so much good humor that Meredith grinned. "Maybe his name ain't Bill," Sarrett said. "You know how those dodgers are . . . always getting details wrong." His amused gray eyes watched Meredith a moment. "That's right, Sam, make sure Betters don't have another gun hid out somewhere."

After a while Meredith decided the carbine and the empty shotgun seemed to be the size of things. He threw the carbine as far as he could.

Sarrett pointed upgrade with his six-gun. "Thank you, gentlemen, and good bye!"

They were riding hard for purple hills north of the river when lead sang past and they heard the rifle at the top of Gypsum Hill.

"Told you that Betters was tricky," Sarrett said. "He had a long-gun roped somewhere under the coach. Spread!"

The next shot was short, but Betters had the line all right and the line was right at Meredith. It always seemed to be that way, but this time it was probably because his Mexican sorrel made a better target at a distance than Sarrett's gray. He bent low in the saddle and rode, waiting for the next shot.

Sarrett laughed. He laughed any old time, with sand blowing in his face, when he was hungry, with a gun in his guts. "Over there," he said. "The heroes of Hallidane are spurring to the kill."

Riders drawn by shots were stringing dust from town. Only one went toward the coach; the others cut toward Meredith and Sarrett.

"Lots of fun at one of those riding bees," Sarrett said.

Betters's third shot made Meredith's horse lunge ahead with a snort. Meredith looked over the leather-covered box under his right arm. The sorrel's rump was bright with blood coming from a streak where the bullet had angled maybe an inch deep.

A minute later they were into a sandy dip and far out of range.

"All right?" Sarrett asked.

"Not good," Meredith said. "Now both me and the sorrel are shot in the rump."

It wasn't really as funny as Sarrett took it.

It wasn't funny at all when the sorrel began to weaken just a little and the riders behind held on.

"Stick to this wash," Sarrett said. "I'll swing to the left and take 'em off your tail. See you at Elfego's place tomorrow night."

Before he put his gray lunging up the bank, Sarrett took the leather box with a casual jerk of his arm.

"Wait a minute! Half of that. . . ."

"Half and the price of a new horse, Brett. Right now you got to ride light. Elfego's tomorrow night. You can find it all right?"

There wasn't time to argue. "I can find it," Meredith said. Later he heard shots and yells from a long way west, so he knew that Sarrett had gone in close enough to make it interesting.

Meredith reached Elfego's place just after sundown the day after Gypsum Hill. On the edge of the brush, the sprawling collection of weathered adobe seemed at the moment to be inhabited only by naked children, goats, and chickens. There was an excuse for a corral straddling a little stream. Meredith knew Elfego had other corrals somewhere back in the tangled brasada.

A brown lad about fourteen, silver spurs on his bare feet, tremendous buckteeth in his mouth, and lots of *sabe* in his liquid eyes, took the Mexican sorrel, glanced at the crusted edges of the wound where vicious flies had gathered, and went toward the brush after nodding toward the largest building.

The buckshot wound felt worse when Meredith started to walk than it had when he was riding. He'd had one canteen of water since yesterday, and he'd used most of it to sponge the sorrel's mouth and nostrils. The sun had burned

14

through the top of his riddled hat and got to his skull in spite of his thick hair. He took the hat off and rubbed a dusty sleeve against his forehead.

There was a hundred dollar note under the band of that hat. Sarrett had one just like it. It was only common sense, Sarrett always said, to carry a little reserve and never spend it. That way you were never broke. There would be plenty of notes to carry as soon as Sarrett got here. They could rest their horses until morning and then ride on.

Damn the sun and damn his thirst, Meredith thought as he shook his head to clear it. He stepped over crawling children and dusty hens and went into the largest adobe.

Elfego was eating goat stew by himself at a table in the middle of the sprinkled floor. He was naked to the waist, but he had his peaked straw hat on, with the greasy bangs of his curly hair shining darkly against sweat. *"Señor!"* he exclaimed, and pointed to a chair, and went right on eating goat stew.

Meredith had a glass of wine that didn't help his thirst at all. Elfego saw. His big innocent eyes were seeing much. He yelled in Spanish and spewed fragments of peppery stew halfway across the table. An old woman came in with a jug of warm water. About half of it and Meredith thought he felt a little better, even if it didn't take the sun out of his head. He ate some of the goat stew and had to drink the rest of the water quickly.

"And now," Elfego said some time later, raking delicately between large teeth with a Bowie knife that had crusted blood and goat hair against the hilt, "you have come to visit my poor house. Welcome, *señor!*"

"How much?" Meredith asked. Sarrett always waited to the end and then paid twice as much as if he'd bargained in the beginning. "I'll want a lead horse, too . . . and not one of those scrubs that go blind as soon as they're led out of the brush."

"Money, *señor?* Money?" Elfego picked his teeth with one hand and spread the other as if the subject was very boring. "Later, *señor.* I see you do not sit well, on the one side only. A little accident, perhaps?"

"Nothing." The chunk of buck was paining like the devil and his whole thigh was sore.

From the next building came deep laughter, the musical laughter of Mexican girls, and the squeals of children that had been amused by something. Sarrett was probably here already, Meredith thought. People laughed like that when he was around. Even with the detour he had taken, he should have been here first. The long-legged gray was a ground-comber.

"Jack Sarrett over there?" Meredith inclined his head.

Elfego sucked his lips. "Sarrett? Sarrett? Names, *señor,* they are nothing at Elfego's."

"A gray horse, no silver on the saddle. A big man with hair like yours. He laughs so that you would not forget." What was the use of talking? Meredith would see for himself. He started to rise.

"That one?" Something quick and thoughtful ran in Elfego's eyes. "No, he is not here." The thought ran on after his words stopped.

"He will be, tonight."

"Perhaps," Elfego said. He ticked the point of his knife up and down against the table. "Now we will talk about money, *señor.*"

Meredith didn't like the quick change, the insinuation. Where did this stack of lard get the right to hint that Sarrett wouldn't make the rendezvous? "Tonight will be soon enough," he said.

16

"Now, perhaps," Elfego said politely.

Meredith's chair was clear of the table. He had room to move and he was already leaning a little sidewise to keep weight off his wound. He lifted his right hand off the chair arm. "Tonight, I said."

Elfego shrugged. "Tonight. The house of Elfego is peaceful. We are simple people here."

And so was anyone who trusted Elfego, Meredith thought. He took a drink of wine and tried to drink away his dizziness.

Elfego cut the piece of buckshot out that night, using his all-purpose knife. Of course, he was not skilled, but he was quick and not afraid of cutting.

"Would you like to keep the lead, *señor?*" he asked. "It is not a great piece, but. . . ."

"Hell, no!" Meredith said, and grunted when Elfego poured tequila into the gash.

Lying on his stomach on a low, flat roof, Meredith watched the moon come up large. Liquid Spanish and soft music flowed gently, murmuring to the dusk. The complaints of sleepy children died away.

Deep laughter mingled with the sounds of women's voices. There were several women here, and few were old. "My wife's cousins, I think," Elfego had said. "So many children, people . . . one cannot remember everything."

Meredith had seen the men, too, longriders like himself. Sarrett was not among them.

When the wash of moonlight began to die, still Sarrett had not come. Meredith drowsed uneasily there on the roof, with his gun beside him. The night was cool, but he was hot. Nothing moved on the trail he watched. Toward dawn Elfego's place was quiet. The roof was cold then.

Sarrett had not come. *He might have got hit drawing the pursuers off,* Meredith thought, *or he might have been forced to lay low somewhere else. He will be here.*

Elfego woke him when the light was gray. The Mexican was standing below, at the end of the building. From near the brush came the sounds of footsteps and a soft curse as men moved away into the thickets.

Meredith's hat was right where he had left it, with his arm across it.

"You will ride now," Elfego said. "The sheriff comes from Hallidane with men."

Meredith came down from the roof. He was burning with fever and shaking at the same time. "I'll wait for Sarrett."

"*Sí, sí!* But not at my poor *jacal*. If you stay, you must wait in the Pit."

Meredith had heard of the Pit, a hole scooped out somewhere back in the brush. It was said that two wounded men hidden there by Elfego had been torn to pieces by javelinas.

"Not the Pit."

Elfego kept glancing into the grayness. "If you cannot ride, there is no other place. The sheriff sometimes leaves men here for three days. Like pigs they eat. It is a small price I must pay. . . ."

"I want a lead horse, a good one. The sorrel will be stiff for a while. . . ."

"You have money?"

"Damn you, no! But later. . . ."

"I could trade her for the sorrel, but . . . ah, the poor horse! So badly wounded. . . ."

"The hell it is! In a week's time. . . ."

"The horse may die soon." Elfego sighed. "But I am a

generous man. I, Elfego, will trade my best mare for this poor dying sorrel only because. . . ."

The noise of distant hoofs came from the trail that led toward the plains.

"The sorrel and fifty dollars," Elfego said.

"I'll stay and fight it out with the sheriff," Meredith said. The way he felt he didn't care.

Elfego groaned. "My best mare gone for a crippled horse. This is what happens when a poor man. . . ."

"Move!" Meredith ordered.

They did not go all the way to the corral. In a small open space a few hundred feet back in the brush the same buck-toothed boy who had led the sorrel away was waiting with a saddled mare, a pot-bellied sabina.

"My poor Conchita, my lovely horse, I grieve. . . ." Elfego put his arms around the mare's neck and she staggered.

It was the worst kind of robbery. Meredith drew his gun. "We'll go to the corral," he said.

From the house a deep voice ran out over the thickets. "Tom! Take two men in to check the corrals. They'll be moved again, but have a look."

Time had run out. Meredith swung up on the sabina and the animal sighed at the weight.

"Go north, *señor,*" Elfego said. "Go with God."

"Go to hell!" Meredith said, and rode off in a warped saddle on a rack of bones. The buck-toothed lad had already slipped away to take the sorrel where no posse would find it.

The pink mare had dropped somewhere from old age and exhaustion, and Meredith was stumbling through agrito, trying to curse, his body a world of fever and weariness, when he remembered one bright thing from the whole mess—the hundred dollar note. Catclaw raked his back as he slumped down to have a look. His hands were big and fumbly, unusually slow for *his* hands. His clothes were torn. His eyes were red-hot and sheets of grayness kept rushing across his vision.

It was a long time before he knew he didn't have the note. Gone with everything else, stolen while he lay asleep on Elfego's roof so long ago.

He stumbled on, with thorns ripping and sticking in flesh where other thorns had already ripped and stuck. There was only one way, just cover your face with your arms and bull ahead. He fell and tasted blood on his arms where flies were working. His gun was a terrible weight, but he wouldn't drop it. He didn't dare drop it.

Where ghost-gray trees stood gauntly around a blinding open space, he fell and crawled, and then he could not crawl any more.

Elfego was stealing his gun, the last thing he had of any value. Meredith tried to fight him off, but he couldn't talk and he couldn't see. And suddenly it was all over.

He woke up four days later. He saw pecan ceiling beams above him and through a large window set in stone the blunt rise and fall of the brasada with the setting sun on it.

"Well, stranger, I thought you were young and tough."

There was an old man in the low-ceilinged room, a stringy old cuss with bright brown eyes that moved as quickly as a roadrunner. Maybe he wasn't so old, at that, Meredith decided after he had a better look. It was just that the mark of the brush was on him, the same lean, tough, weathered look that grows on a brush-popping steer.

"Picked you up in the salt bed on my way from town,"

the old boy said. "Have a drink of this." It was *huisache* tea, and Meredith was to drink a lot of it before he could defend himself.

"Town?" he asked.

"Mesa Vaca."

That was a long way from Hallidane, at least. Meredith closed his eyes again. Later that evening the old man fed him some wild *chiltipiquines*. "Best thing in the world for fever, or anything else. You had a bad time, son, even after I got you here."

Meredith knew that when he tried to get up the next day and couldn't make it.

He stayed almost a month with old Andy McRae. At first he thought any man who would live alone in this place was crazy—ticks and heat and thickets all around, and wild bulls that bellowed in the evening at the water hole below the stone house. McRae owned two thousand acres of brush and he didn't know how many steers, nor was it likely that all the riders in Texas could ever have choused them out to tally.

Later, Meredith decided that the place wasn't too bad. It was cool sometimes in the evening. If a man got to know the brush . . . well, maybe after you got as old as McRae, it might be all right.

"I'll be drifting in a day or two, Andy," he said one night. He had to find Sarrett, who would be looking for him, too, get his share of the loot from Gypsum Hill—and then he'd try to pay old Andy for what he'd done.

"Sure, son." Andy sucked his pipe and nodded. Then he got up and took a piece of paper from a cupboard. As dodgers go, it was a good picture of Meredith and Sarrett standing together at a hitch rack before a Comanche Wells saloon. Sarrett had been laughing at the way the traveling photographer went under his dusty black cloth. The dodger said Sarrett was worth three hundred dollars more than Meredith.

"Quite a boy, that Sarrett," McRae said. "The day after him and . . . somebody . . . outfoxed Clyde Betters at Gypsum Hill, Sarrett took a stage west of Comanche for thirteen thousand dollars."

"West of Comanche!" Meredith stared into McRae's lively brown eyes. That meant that Sarrett had ridden like the very devil to get there the day after Gypsum Hill.

"It was a well-planned business," McRae said, and went on to describe it.

After a few moments Meredith wasn't listening. That second robbery had been set up at least a week in advance, from what McRae said. Sarrett never had intended to go to Elfego's. "Right now you got to ride light," he'd said when he took the money. Sure, he'd led the posse away from Meredith, but he'd had to cross their route anyway to get where he'd been headed all the time.

Anger thumped and churned in Meredith. There wasn't a ten-year-old kid in Texas half as simple as he'd been. Elfego had known all the time after Sarrett's name was mentioned. Sitting there, belching at his table, he'd been able to guess the truth in a second. Meredith thought of the hours he'd spent lying on the roof, watching, waiting, afraid that Sarrett had run into hard luck.

And then on top of everything, Elfego had pulled *his* whizzer. But Sarrett was the cause of it all.

"Got it all figured out?" McRae asked.

"Including the killing."

"Big order, of course," McRae said mildly. "The last the Rangers heard of Sarrett he'd crossed into Oklahoma. They got the man that took the big chance on the job west of Comanche. Got him the hard way."

"Naturally they got him," Meredith said bitterly. "Can you trust me for a saddle and horse?"

"We can fix up something. I been trading around a little while you were learning to walk. . . ." He stopped when he saw how Meredith resented a glance at his thigh.

The next day he took Meredith back into the brush a piece. McRae, also, had a corral not too close to his house. In it was Meredith's Mexican saddle and bridle. McRae looked embarrassed. "I know Elfego pretty well, know how to straighten him out now and then. I . . . well . . . there's your damned stuff, kid. The sorrel's good as ever now."

What Elfego had done to Meredith didn't seem so important now. Greed walks with any man. But Sarrett—he had made a damned fool of a friend. "You got to ride light," he'd said, and he'd been laughing to himself.

"You know," McRae said, "I'd just forget about Sarrett. Say you were lucky enough to catch him and fast enough to blast him . . . it wouldn't do you any good. He'd go out laughing at you. That's the way he's made."

"You know him?"

"He's stopped here. I never seen a man I liked as much and trusted as little as Jack Sarrett. Take that business of carrying a hundred dollar bill in his hat. He never did in his life. He spends money so fast he never even gets it into his pockets, let alone in his hat. But he's talked plenty of suckers into carrying a big bill in their hats just so's he or somebody else could steal it when the time was right."

Meredith was glad McRae was looking into the catclaw at the moment.

"No," McRae said, "killing him wouldn't give a man much satisfaction . . . and it would be a big order, too."

"Every wolf has its bullet."

"I wouldn't bother with him, son."

"Thanks . . . for advice I don't need."

"I didn't either, when I was your age," McRae said. "Going after him ain't a question of what it's going to do for him . . . it's a question of what it's going to do to you."

Meredith didn't understand and he didn't care to. He said: "I'll take care of myself."

Before he crossed the Brazos he was doubly sure his way was best. A long day's ride always pained him—the results of Betters's shotgun. Elfego's filthy knife, and Sarrett's double-cross were concentrated in one place. While no man watching him ride could have guessed he pained, whenever Meredith went up in the saddle he was reminded that he must seek vengeance.

It was worse than mangled ears that showed a gunslinger had made a fool of you. You could wear your ears down the street in plain sight and let your eyes dare any man to look too long or make a crack.

In Fort Worth he knocked a saddle maker off the walk when the man, after watching Meredith get stiffly from his horse, suggested that the saddle didn't fit him.

He crossed the Big Red and, at a small tent town on Little Red, got his first news of Sarrett. Crooked land speculators had worked railroad talk to a frenzy and had reaped a fine harvest selling lots the month before. And then the assistant to the chief surveyor of the railroad arrived, got chummy with the speculators, and for an undisclosed sum tipped them off to exactly where the railroad was going to run.

The speculators rushed south to the promised land and bought up the farms of two startled farmers who had just about starved out. There were even a few survey stakes around to sustain the wild buying. Immediately the assistant to the chief surveyor, a big, curly-haired man who laughed a lot and spent money freely, went away to get his parties organized and working full swing.

It was some time before the speculators learned that they had cornered land in a country where no railroad ever would run.

"You'd've laughed yourself sick to hear them sharks howl," a bartender told Meredith. "Can't say as I blame 'em for being took in, either. This Meredith was a man I'd 'a' trusted. . . ."

"Who?"

"Brett Meredith, the fellow as said he was the surveyor. Looked like a longhorn to me."

"Yeah," Meredith said, and drank his whiskey at a gulp, sand and all. "Yeah, I guess I would have laughed myself sick. I wonder where this . . . Meredith . . . went from here?"

"Nobody knows." The bartender blew some of the sand off a dirty glass and set it on the plank bar. "But a man like that will be heard from again, I'll bet."

Meredith didn't know which way to go. He sort of favored Texas, figuring that by now Sarrett had slipped back. Rangers wouldn't worry him too much. They never had.

The twenty dollars McRae had given him had taken him a long way, but he was flat now. Buzzer, the Mexican sorrel, had to eat and so did Brett Meredith. He took a dry, empty stomach a long way to where he'd heard of a trail drive. Tol Carruthers, the top screw, looked him over and said he didn't need any hands. "That is, unless"—the drover boss shook his head doubtfully—"you wanted to take the wagon. The cook's rheumatics put him flat two weeks ago on the other side of the Red. It was mainly just not wanting to leave Texas, I think."

"I'll take it," Meredith said, and that was another disgrace to score against Sarrett, who was somewhere fat as a feeder steer and laughing his head off. "Where in Kansas?"

"To the Platte . . . that's up in Nebraska." Carruthers looked at the way Meredith wore his gun. "Never been out of Texas before, huh?"

"That," said Meredith, "is none of your damned business."

"You sound like a cook already," the foreman said. "Camp in an hour. We're going to be mighty hungry."

Meredith was mighty hungry at the moment. It was probably colder than Alaska up in Nebraska, but it might be as good a place as any to look for Sarrett.

By the time he'd crossed Kansas, he had almost learned to cook. He took a lot of ragging, not all good-natured, about his efforts. He took nothing the morning he rolled from under the wagon with his hip hurting from a night in blankets soaked by rain that had washed up against him.

"Got lead in your pants this morning, Gimpy?" Hod Oliver asked.

Meredith took off his apron. His cedar-handled Colt was where he always wore it, even while cooking. He faced Oliver and the rest eating around the fire. "What was that you asked?"

They looked at his blocky face and his narrowed eyes. Oliver had trouble swallowing a mouthful of flapjacks. "No offense, Cookie," he said. "I pass the hand."

For Texans, they were even careful in the remarks they made about his cooking after that.

Meredith was surprised to find no snow in Nebraska in early September. In fact, he thought it hotter there than many parts of Texas. Folks in the little railroad town where the drive ended were laughing about something that had happened over at Ryepatch that summer. A saloon man there had paid eight dollars a head for a thousand steers, received a bill of sale, and taken a couple of drinks when the seller set up the house to celebrate the deal. The only hitch was that the cattle bedded down just a quarter of a mile away had not belonged to the seller.

"What did the feller look like?" Meredith asked a bartender.

"Like the man who owned the herd. He rode right over from the drive while the others was getting the steers bedded down, only it turns out later that he'd been riding with 'em only a few miles. Well, anyone sucker enough to think he could buy at eight dollars a head. . . ."

Meredith drew half his pay. He told Carruthers to send the rest to a man named Andy McRae at Mesa Vaca when the Texans got as close as they would go to the place.

Carruthers said: "It gets mighty cold up here, I've heard."

"I can stand it, if he can."

Carruthers didn't ask who. He said: "I thought it was like that. See you in Texas, kid."

The saloonkeeper in Ryepatch was very sour about the mess he'd stepped into, but he had to justify his error. "This Clyde Betters had the marks of the long haul all over him. He was dry, too." The saloon man shook his head at Meredith. "A man comes in here with a herd bawling and kicking dust so close I could have hit 'em with an empty bottle. He says he owns that herd and wants to do business before he gets so drunk he ain't responsible. These yahoos around here are laughing now, but not one of them that was here at the time and drunk the whiskey this Betters set up for 'em thought he was anything but what. . . ."

"A big black-haired man, laughed with his eyes so you had to laugh with him, gray eyes?"

"That's him!" The saloon man added darkly: "A friend of yours?"

"No friend of mine."

"I'll stand a drink on that. I need one every time I think about him."

"Any idea which way this . . . Betters . . . went?"

The saloon man grunted and gave the question the silence it deserved.

Meredith sat into a stud game. He needed enough money to finance his search for a while without having to be slowed down by working. In a half hour he was broke. There wasn't much to being honest, he thought. He got his horse and ground-hitched it at the side of the bank. They were shoveling around a lot of money in there. Just a couple of pocketfuls out of the teller's window near the door would be all he needed.

He rolled a cigarette and waited for customers to clear out of the bank. People shuffling through the dust didn't pay much attention to him until a little man with eyes like Clyde Betters's walked up and stuck a gun in his back. *Suspicious people here in Nebraska,* Meredith thought. He hadn't even robbed the bank yet.

Across the street another man with a badge stepped out from between two buildings. He had a rifle.

The marshal behind Meredith said: "You seen the sign that says Texans don't carry guns in Ryepatch?"

"No," Meredith lied, and breathed easier.

"Too bad," the marshal said.

The marshal wasn't downright mean. After Meredith got out of jail sometime later, he helped the Texan find a job on a ranch forty miles west on the river. It was the worst winter

Meredith ever put in. The longhorns drifted into fence corners, piled up and froze, and Meredith almost died, in spite of shotgun chaps, a woman's shawl under his hat, and—worst of all—bulky overshoes on top of his boots. His wound ached something fierce every time he got into a frosty saddle. Buzzer didn't like the winter either.

Oh, Lord! What an awful score there was against Jack Sarrett.

Sometimes in spite of himself Meredith jerked open the door of the miserable sod hut they called a line shanty in this north country and stared into blizzards to see if he really had heard Sarrett laughing out there. But he knew Jack Sarrett had not been trapped in the cold, not him. He was in some warm *cantina,* far away from air that struck like a knife.

Spring came at last and there wasn't a bluebonnet in sight, just sand and dirty brown grass.

In Ryepatch Meredith got half of his winter's wages changed into one note. He gave a milliner a dollar to put some oiled silk around it and sew it under the sweatband of his hat. He'd break into that hundred dollars to celebrate right after he gunned Jack Sarrett kicking.

Here and there on his way toward the Red, Meredith saw Wanted sheets with the same picture McRae had shown him in the brasada. He was glad that he'd only trimmed the beard he'd grown for warmth that winter in the snow.

Down in the southern hills of Oklahoma, where people said the winter had been mild, a big, popular laughing man named Starr had run a saloon for a few weeks until, tiring of it, he had given it to the bartender and ridden away, singing. The women in the town, married and unmarried, had thought well of Starr, even if he had been a saloonkeeper.

Not far from the Texas line Meredith made up to a dance-hall woman to see if he couldn't get some news of Sarrett. She didn't know or wouldn't talk about the man, but she did warm up to Meredith enough to warn him that two tough deputy sheriffs were just about to snap up a red-headed man who owned a Mexican sorrel.

It was close. Buzzer split a lot of Texas air before Meredith got back across the line. He got to figuring that, if he, who hadn't owned much of a record at all before he joined up with Sarrett, could attract so much lawdog lead, Sarrett would be good for much more. The laughing man was no fool in spite of his arrogant carelessness.

He was probably letting crime in Texas limp along without him.

Out in western Oklahoma Meredith heard about the stage that had been robbed in a gully east of Red Feather that spring. At dusk one evening the stage had come against large rocks piled across the road where a sign burned into a wagon board said: **BRIDGE BUSTED**.

The guard, driver, and passengers argued about the sign and the bridge half a mile away. In the end, the driver followed a promising detour because it showed fresh marks of several wagons. The stage was robbed of fifteen thousand dollars after it was hopelessly stuck in a gully. No one got a look at the man in the dark, but everyone heard him laugh as he gave orders to four confederates stationed with rifles along the sides of the trap. Some passengers said seven confederates.

Daylight showed the tracks of only one horse—and three piles of brush that had been set against the skyline to look like men with rifles. Daylight also showed a broken-down wagon that had been run many times over the false detour, making it look well traveled.

Sarrett must have really laughed about that one, Meredith thought grimly. He was beginning to worry about Sarrett a little. The man would make a mistake and get killed.

Reliable information from people who were authorities on the Red Feather job indicated seven directions in which Meredith's man had gone.

A cowboy with a rusty-red thatch of hair, a short beard, and a look in his eye came into Granada, Colorado, that fall on a Mexican sorrel with a gray scar welt on its rump. He watched other cowboys welcome in a train by trying to shoot the headlight out, and learned that Curly Elfego, a laughing man from Oklahoma, had introduced the pastime one day when things were dull.

It was also in Granada, when two saloon men were warning verbally, threatening to blow each other's places sky-high, that someone rolled an immense, spitting bomb into the Plains Palace one night. Windows and closed doors and other fragile barriers that impeded egress went out with the crowd, and soon the palace was deserted except for a dance-hall girl who had been knocked under a table and who was too scared to move but scared enough to remember a prayer.

The bomb made a lot of smoke that fogged the interior. The dance-hall girl, between prayers, watched Curly Elfego moving unhurriedly but efficiently as he raked into a gunnysack abandoned money from the cashier's doghouse and the bar tills. Later, the girl forgot her praying and used other language that came more naturally. She threw a pail of beer on the bomb, which turned out to be a large, black-painted wooden ball with a burned-out fuse.

Again, Meredith had his choice of many directions. He was a month behind.

The man who stopped beside Meredith in front of the Queen one night had all the looks of a smoky trail behind him, a tight mouth, wary eyes, and a face that was not easy to read.

"Looking for a man?" he asked.

"I didn't say so."

"No, but for two days you've sure swiveled your ears like a deer when a certain name was mentioned."

Meredith's face and eyes were hard.

"I figured I was about two thousand ahead when Curly Elfego rolled that phony bomb into the Palace," the man said. "Only time I ever won in my whole life. I picked up my chips, but, by the time I got out, I'd been shoved and tromped so much I didn't have a single counter left."

"Too bad."

"Yeah, only I mean it. This Curly . . . I heard him tell a woman he was on his way to Juárez. Had a deal there. Said he could pass as a Mex when he wanted to."

"I didn't ask about Curly Elfego," Meredith said. He thought he knew a blazer when he heard one.

"You sure didn't," the man said, and started away.

"Who was the woman?" Meredith asked.

"Pearl. The only good-looking one at the Queen."

She was that, all right. Meredith already had tried to pump her about Sarrett, and got nowhere at all. Women were like that after Jack Sarrett had passed through their lives. This time he didn't rush things. Down on the Pecos nobody had called him an open-mouthed jinglebob around women from the time he was sixteen.

He sold the lead horse he'd picked up on his way across Kansas and spent almost all of the money on Pearl. He had three fights before a few hardheads admitted he was the fair-haired boy for the moment. She liked him, too, he decided. She even told him the giveaway signs of a blackjack dealer at the Queen, so he was able to make several minor killings and buy the lead horse back. Pearl talked him into shaving his beard, and he didn't mind that, either, because he was a long way from the last dodger he'd seen with his picture on it.

But he couldn't waste too much time. One night he asked: "I wonder where old Curly ever went from here?"

Pearl stiffened just a little, and then she got a sort of dreamy look in her eye, like a lot of women who had known Sarrett.

"I guess he drifted back to Nebraska, probably," Meredith said.

"I suppose. He said he always liked it there."

Meredith knew he wasn't going to get any place playing the edges. Pearl was pretty fond of him in her way, and she couldn't know who he was, so he jumped right into the middle. "Did he ever mention going to Juárez?"

If he hadn't been watching so closely, he never would have seen the flick of caution in her eyes or her split-second hesitation. "No," she said. "He mentioned going lots of places, but I'm sure Juárez wasn't one of them."

It was good enough for Meredith. He rode south that afternoon with enough money to see him through. No one in Raton was very communicative, but finally a stable hostler admitted that a big, laughing man with curly black hair had been there the month before.

In Las Vegas, Meredith had to go into Old Town and take his chances before he found a loafer who had seen Sarrett only three weeks before. Because it offered a large field for Sarrett's talent, Albuquerque was probably the man's next stop, Meredith reasoned. So he cut southwest, instead, to see if he couldn't pick up time.

He had a rough two weeks on Chupadera Mesa, got lost, nearly died of thirst, took an Apache arrow in the arm, and lost his lead horse. But nothing could stop him now. Even Buzzer, gaunt and weary, seemed to know that at last they were closing.

Meredith reached Lava Butte. He was thin, grim, and dried out like old leather. No one in Lava Butte admitted they had seen this man.

The sheriff at Las Cruces, almost to the border, sized Meredith up keenly during his first half hour in town. He looked at the sorrel and seemed satisfied.

"You're Brett Meredith, ain't you?" he asked.

Meredith nodded, his mind and muscles ready. He'd never shot a badge-toter yet, but nobody was going to stop him.

"Got a message for you," the sheriff said. "C'mon."

Meredith went warily. The officer took a dirty piece of paper from a desk drawer and handed it over.

BRIDGE OUT, it read, **but since you've gone that far, why not visit Juárez anyway?** It was signed: **Jack**.

"Mex riding through give it to me last week," the lawman said to him very slowly.

For a while Meredith wouldn't believe what he knew was sure. All he could think of was about the Apaches that had almost got him, of days without water, and of how Sarrett must be laughing. He choked as he asked: "This Mex . . . what did he look like?"

"Maybe fifty, go 'bout a hundred and ten, spoke fair English. . . ." He watched Meredith sink into a chair. "Too much sun, maybe?"

Meredith was sick all right. It had been a typical Sarrett trick from scratch. That tight-mouthed man in Granada couldn't have made it stick alone . . . but Pearl . . . she'd cinched it with just a tiny bit of acting. And these people he thought he'd so cleverly searched out along the way—they'd been paid off by the little Mexican to keep Meredith going. Sarrett was laughing himself sick.

The sheriff, of course, didn't understand, but he was sympathetic. "Lots of officers have missed by closer than you, son."

Being called a lawman piled on more than Meredith thought he could bear. He staggered outside where the hot strike of the afternoon sun reminded him again of what he'd been through.

"Better rest up," the sheriff said. "You're fearful gaunted. What's the matter there with your rear? You keep rubbing. . . ."

"I got it caught in a bear trap!" Meredith said savagely. "When I was poking into other folks' business."

He left without filling his canteens, but after a few miles he realized he wasn't going back to Granada at that pace.

It took him five months to get back. He had to work where he could, once on a railroad carrying green ties with Mexican laborers. He never thought of spending the hundred in his hat—a different hat now. That money was still for celebrating right after his wolf had caught its bullet.

Long ago he had ruled against using his guns for easy passage. Three weeks in the Ryepatch jail had taught him how bad it would be if he slipped on a job and was put away somewhere to reflect for years on a mission unfulfilled.

Pearl was still at the Queen when Meredith rode into Granada one bitter day with the wind whipping dust and dry snow against his ragged clothes.

Her face got a little pale, but her eyes were unafraid. She

shrugged away a tall cowboy, who stepped a little farther aside when he saw Meredith's face. She led Meredith to her room to talk, and they did not speak a word on the way. He'd never beaten a woman the way he was going to beat her. He'd slapped down wildcats in *cantinas* when they had tried to knife him, but this had to be better than a casual wallop.

"You might have found him if I hadn't helped send you down there," she said, so matter-of-factly that he was stopped for a moment. "I don't know what it is that sends you after Jack Sarrett, but I know it can't be worth it to you. It's made you so bitter you aren't young."

"You helped age me." He'd spent his twenty-third birthday on Chupadera, beside a dead horse, with Apaches trying to work in to finish him. "You helped do that! You lied to me. You lied to me!"

"I lied, of course, but not for money like the rest. The twelve days I knew Jack Sarrett meant something to me that you couldn't understand. I was never so happy and laughed so much in my life . . . and I knew all the time he'd ride away when he wanted to. And if I knew where he was right now, I'd lie to you again."

She grabbed a two-barreled Derringer from under a dirty pillow and stood with it at her side. "Now, if you're still set on showing what a big fierce man you are . . . start!"

She wasn't bluffing, he knew. He also knew he could get her wrist before she had the Derringer all the way up.

"So you love the no good son!" he snarled.

"That's none of your damned business! At least, he never set out to kill a man. You're a dirty killer at heart, Brett Meredith. Jack's just out for the laughs there are in life."

She sat down on the bed suddenly and let the gun drop on a scrap of dust-covered faded green carpet. Here and there she'd made a stab to pretty up the place, but it was just like a hundred other rooms Meredith had seen in places like the Queen.

He drew a deep breath and glared at her. She wasn't even looking at him now, just sitting there with her mouth screwed up, her face not very clean, her eyes staring at the floor. Even then she was a handsome girl, and she was younger than he, but there wasn't much chance that she'd be either young or good-looking very long.

She'd lied about Sarrett to Meredith, and now for the rest of her life she'd lie to herself about those twelve days with Jack Sarrett. Meredith knew that as he stood there with his eyes bloodshot from dust and cold, with his hard, whiskered jaw tightening his mouth. He told himself he ought to knock her around until she couldn't go out on the floor for a month.

But all he did was walk from the room and leave her sitting there, staring at a faded scrap of carpet in a dirty, cold room where wind was pushing sand past warping window frames.

He stopped in a town on the Arkansas where rattlesnakes outnumbered other inhabitants, a town with a brand new church that had been donated by a traveling minister named Jonathan Starr.

"He was a handsome man with a vital, stirring appearance," a woman member of the congregation told Meredith, "and he wasn't afraid of an honest laugh. Of course, when we discovered that the lumber he donated for the church really belonged to the Santa Fé railroad, it was embarrassing." She rallied and went on staunchly. "But I'm sure Reverend Starr confused the pile with some that he had ordered."

"Uhn-huh, so am I. And where is the Reverend Starr now, do you know?"

"He said he was going north to carry the message to Blackfoot Indians in Montana."

Lord help the Blackfeet! Meredith thought as he mounted his horse.

Montana was a long ride away. Meredith didn't get there until spring. His man had been in Hardin in the fall. A saloon man, who had fallen for the old buried Spanish treasure trick, testified to that.

It was a long time later before Meredith again heard of Sarrett. He was riding shotgun on a stageline out of Larned, making a living and hoping that someday the right robber would step out to make his play. Meredith had gone Clyde Betters one better. In spring clips on the floor of the stage, he'd rigged a carbine and practiced until he could use his toe to flip it into his hands in no time if he ever needed backing for his shotgun.

Meredith was in love with Mary Linford then, daughter of the stageline owner.

She'd been alone in the office the day he'd dropped in to look at pictures in the hope of finding news of Sarrett. He was dusty and his clothes were in bad shape, and never in his life had he been so aware of his appearance than when Mary smiled at him.

"Just wanted to look at the pictures over there, miss."

"Go right ahead," she had said, and smiled again.

He had thumbed past the old one of himself and Sarrett before he realized it. She wasn't like a lot he'd seen, so bright pretty it smacked you right in the face. Her hair was kind of pale blonde and not wavy at all. She was a slender girl and he'd seen many with better curves, or at least more of them. It was her eyes and her smile, some kind of clean-ness that ran all the way through her being.

All at once, even though he knew he was going to ride away soon and never see her again, he had wanted to get rid of the circular of him and Sarrett. He had got it when two men came into the office, one a blunt-jawed man who looked like he could use the gun on his hip, the other a slender youth in dark broadcloth.

The smile that Mary had given the youth was considerably different from the one she'd given Meredith, and it made him look a second time at the young whelp in broadcloth.

"I was thinking, Mary," the youth had said, "that maybe Bart here would do for the guard your father wants."

"He might. Why don't you ask Dad, Roger?"

"Well, you know . . . your word with him. . . ."

"After all, Roger, Dad is the boss."

"I know, but . . . well, all right, we'll ask your father."

The youth was not quite man-size, Meredith had decided. He'd sounded like a kid who wanted to whine a little after his mother refused a favor, but was afraid to.

Meredith had gone over to the counter. "You need a stage guard?"

"Yes." She had sized him up, and he knew that she was seeing plenty.

"I need a job, and I can handle it." Her eyes were the clearest he'd ever seen, a sort of hazel with green flecks in them. They had looked at him for what seemed a long time.

"You're hired," she had said, and only then did she glance at the door and let her eyes say that she trusted him not to shoot off his mouth.

D. C. Linford never knew but that he had done the hiring himself when he came in a half hour later. Meredith wasn't simple enough to think he'd charmed the girl, and he wasn't surprised at all to find out later that Bart was considered unreliable because of whiskey, or that he owed Roger Hammond's father money.

The weeks rolled with the stages. Meredith had enough money to go on with his search, but he told himself he needed more, and, besides, maybe Sarrett would come to him if he just waited long enough.

He didn't exactly dislike Roger Hammond, the only son of one of the town's leading merchants, but he did consider the youth a poor excuse for Mary, even if it was foregone that the two were to be married someday. Hammond wasn't much. He'd have been in the way in Chupadera and other places. But he had the stability of a town around him and money behind him, so maybe he'd be all right.

Meredith got to take Mary to dances several times when Roger was busy at the store. Finally the guard decided that Hammond wasn't going to have her at all. He began to tell himself that Mary's smile carried for him the same message it did for Roger Hammond.

One night, when he was driving her home from a dance out in the country under starlight so bright he could have shot a tomato can at twenty paces, he stopped the buggy and said abruptly: "I've been saving my money."

"I know," she said, "and I think that's fine."

Nothing that had worked with other girls was any good now. The old, easy ways didn't even come to his mind.

"Look, Mary, the day I first saw you there in the office, when you trusted me without asking a single question, I. . . ." He took a deep breath and looked at her face tilted up in the starlight. "I love you, Mary . . . something awful."

"I know." There was a sadness in her voice that chilled him. "I'm going to marry Roger, Brett."

"Why? He hasn't got. . . ." He almost made the mistake

of saying what he thought of Roger Hammond.

"I know he hasn't been hardened by trial as you have. I know you look down on him because he hasn't done the same things as you have. But I love him and I'm going to marry him."

He didn't remember starting the horse. "What's wrong with me, Mary?"

"Nothing. You're as fine a man as I've ever known. Some girl will be mighty lucky. . . ."

Some girl! Lord help him, there was only one girl in the world.

He stopped the horse again. "Look, if it's anything in my past that's hurting me, I'll tell you every. . . ."

"No, Bret. It's nothing in your past, and, if I loved you, I'd marry you and never ask about your past."

"It is my past!"

She shook her head. "No. I told the same thing to Jack Sarrett, and he believed. . . ."

"Jack Sarrett!" He couldn't believe it.

"I'll tell you everything now. He was here last summer. He came into the office his first few minutes in town, just as you did. Only he was sizing things up for a robbery. He told me afterward. Jack Sarrett stayed in Larned all summer and made Roger so jealous he couldn't sleep nights."

"Jack Sarrett wanted to marry you?" Meredith choked back a curse.

"I finally convinced him I was going to marry Roger."

"Why, that Sarrett is the biggest outlaw. . . ."

"I know. He told me everything. He told me about you, too. He said you'd be the bitterest, grimmest man I'd ever seen, and at first I thought he was right, but you've shed a lot of that since you've been here. Don't put it on again, Bret!"

41

"Didn't the marshal . . . somebody . . . recognize . . . ?"

"He's changed a lot since that picture of you two . . . the picture you ripped away your first day here in the office . . . was taken at Comanche Wells. Both of you have changed. Jack Sarrett lived quietly here. He bought a livery stable. He was very well liked and popular."

Before they reached the lights ahead, Meredith stopped the buggy again. "Mary, this Hammond is no man for you. If it ever gets rough after you're married, you're going to have to carry the two of you."

"I know that," she said. "I love him, that's all."

It was all.

Meredith got Buzzer from the stable the next morning. He told D. C. Linford he was leaving. The old man's eyes were wise with knowledge he didn't speak. "You were the best man I ever had," he said. "Come back any time."

Meredith hadn't intended to see Mary again, but he had to. She was alone in the office, just as she'd been that day when dreams that would never be again had started to rise in a dusty, grim man.

"Don't go and wreck your life doing something about a long-ago wrong that doesn't matter now," she told him.

"Will you marry me?"

"Please, Bret, let's not start that again."

"All right. You're the only person in the world that could have stopped me from killing Jack Sarrett, but since you want him killed. . . ."

She didn't say: "You're being foolish." He was and he knew it. She shook her head at him gently and smiled.

"Good bye, Missus Hammond!" he said, and left her. The last he saw of Mary Linford she was standing at the window watching him mount Buzzer.

She waved as he rode away. He did not wave back.

* * * * *

He rode into a loneliness as big as the winds and plains ahead. For a while he hadn't been alone, but now he had no one to talk to, no place to run to for refuge. Days later the worst scalding bitterness was gone, and he wished then that he had been a man those last few moments in the office. He wished, too, that he had smiled and waved at her in leaving.

The only consolation that he had was that Jack Sarrett, for once, had been stopped cold. The filthy, clever son, trying to sell himself to Mary by pretending that he was in love with her. But it hadn't gotten him any place.

For once Meredith could laugh at *him*. But the trouble was he could not laugh at all.

In Dodge City he picked up Sarrett's trail again. This time it led into Wyoming.

Nights crouched beside far campfires with him. Days mocked him with their brightness. He had time to twist his thinking to suit his purpose, and there was no one to challenge his devious reasoning. Long before he reached Cheyenne he had charged his loss of Mary to Sarrett.

Sarrett had been in Cheyenne. He had allowed himself to be drawn into a senseless gunfight and killed two local toughs. The affair puzzled Meredith because it was unlike Jack Sarrett, who had always let force be his tool without actually using it. It was odd, too, that no one seemed to remember Sarrett for his laughing.

In Great Falls, Montana, Meredith lost the trail entirely. It was more than three years before he picked it up again. Necessity trapped him one winter near Fort Benton. Toward spring, when the madness of inaction was upon him, he stood in the doorway of a pole cabin, looking at a snow-locked range with dying cattle, and cursed the weather as he cursed Sarrett, and prayed for a Chinook as he prayed to find Sarrett.

He tried Wyoming again, Nebraska, and Oklahoma, watching the towns where the big drives came through. And then he heard from a man in Kansas that Sarrett was dead.

He couldn't believe it.

He heard it again from a Texan he'd known long before.

"Three, four years back," the fellow said. "The Rangers got him."

Sarrett was dead! Meredith had been robbed. He wasn't quite sane when he began to believe. He got violently drunk in Abilene, and would have killed three men who crossed him. A barkeeper reached out with a shotgun and dented the barrels on Meredith's head. The marshal returned his gun at the edge of town and pointed toward the road. Before Meredith reached Larned on his way to Texas to get the details of Sarrett's death, he bought new clothes.

Old D. C. Linford said that Mary and her husband were now somewhere in Colorado. Hammond's father was dead, the business sold, and the couple had gone to the mountains where Roger was going to make a fortune mining.

"I ain't heard from her in three years," Linford said. "It ain't good with her, or she'd have wrote." He shook his head. "A fellow was here several months back asking about her. Asked about you, too. Jack Sarrett, but when I knew him before his name. . . ."

"Sarrett was here? A few months ago?"

Meredith finally reached the Denver address from which Linford had last heard of his daughter. It was a hotel. Nobody remembered the Hammonds or Sarrett. Again he had hit a blank wall.

Mining, Meredith thought. That's what Hammond had come for. He was somewhere in the mountains, and somewhere close was Sarrett, trailing along, trying to cause trouble, not satisfied with his rebuff.

Meredith didn't like the mountains worth a damn, but where Sarrett went. . . .

Just before spring, at an Indian agency somewhere near the Cochetopa, he was ready to turn back and again try the camps near Denver. The agent said that Zebulon Valley, on west, had no towns and no people except a few fool prospectors that likely had frozen by now.

"Coldest valley in America," the agent said. "Your breath freezes right on your mouth. Last fall the government sent a fellow in there with a hundred head of chunky red and white cattle just to see if they could make it through the winter. The man came past here last month. Said the cattle plumb froze to death. There's grass there, prettiest you ever saw, but that infernal cold. . . ."

"Red and white cattle?" Meredith asked.

"White-faced. I never saw any like 'em before."

Meredith had. Herefords. They didn't freeze easily.

"What did the man look like?"

The description could have fitted Jack Sarrett, an old sort of Sarrett who didn't laugh any more.

Meredith went into Zebulon Valley. The agent had been right about the cold, but where the sun had worked a little, on southern slopes above a river as crooked as bent striped candy, there was bare sage and forage.

He found the carcasses of fifteen steers, and studied them for a long time before he was sure they had been shot instead of frozen to death. In another month no one could have said. It took him three days to find the herd hidden in a feeder valley where they could paw snow for forage. They weren't in bad shape, considering. They had two bulls with them, and there was a good calf crop about due.

Inch by inch Meredith searched the big aspen log cabin he found at the lower end of the valley. It was well stocked with food. It was crudely built, but it was tight. Somebody had spent a lot of time hacking out furniture with an Army-issue axe. He frowned a long time at the second bunk, a small one with a bottom of willows crudely woven. No child had ever used it, because the upraised edges of the dying bark were unbroken.

Just another blind lead, Meredith thought. It was just one of many he'd followed. He'd been right about someone's pulling a sandy on the government. The man had shot a few steers as evidence to back up his report about the herd freezing. In a few weeks he could begin to move them deeper into the mountains, or just leave them where they were.

Any government official stupid enough to believe that Herefords would freeze in this country wouldn't know enough to investigate thoroughly. And to a man who didn't know much, the scattered bones of fifteen steers would look like any number—like one hundred head.

The whole thing smelled like a Sarrett trick, but it was too small, involving too much work. And that little bunk . . . no, he'd followed a bad hunch. He'd rest here overnight and be on his way in the morning.

Soon after the heat of the tiny cook stove hit him, he was terribly drowsy. He went out and took care of Buzzer. There was nothing to do but turn him loose and let him forage with the cattle.

Meredith didn't eat himself. He stoked the fire and lay down on the big bunk, with his gun under the sheepskin coat he was using as a pillow. These failures were coming to hit him harder and harder, now that there was no special urgency to finish Sarrett before he spoiled Mary's life.

The picture started years ago at Andy McRae's corral in the brasada was grooved deeply in Meredith's brain: finding Jack Sarrett, calling to him, watching him turn. Then he'd remind Sarrett of why he was going to die. The rest was a beautiful explosion of savagery, a vision so clear that it had brought Meredith from sleep many times, his teeth gritted, his hand holding a smoking, bucking gun so real that he'd had to look hard to know it was not there.

He was sound asleep in the heat when someone kicked open the door and walked in. Meredith had his gun and was off the bunk before he knew more than that a man was in the room.

Blinding snow glare was all around the man, so that Meredith could scarcely see his lower body. But the fellow's head was well above the top of the open door, where the glare from outside did not hide anything. His hat was dragged down tight over a ragged shawl that Jack Sarrett would not have used to wipe down a lathered horse. Frost was just starting to melt on an unkempt black beard. But nothing could change the gray eyes and the set of the wide mouth.

There he stood, the man who had made Meredith's life a bitter, searching hell, the man who had laughed at him for years. A hundred triumphant, blazing words ran in Meredith's brain. He couldn't say them all at once.

"You're mine, you dirty son!" he finally said.

Sarrett just stood there with the cold fog rolling around him from the open doorway. Meredith didn't have to see more than his face, for his gun knew where to send its churning lead.

"Remember me, Sarrett?"

"I knew you were here, Brett, when I saw the same old Mexican sorrel out there with the cattle. About nine years old now, ain't he?"

Smooth Sarrett was, like always, ready to talk himself out of any crack. His hands would be stiff from cold. He wanted a little time. That was fine. That was the way Meredith had always seen it. Jack Sarrett would get an even chance.

"Pull that door shut with your foot!"

Sarrett hooked the door shut with his foot. The glare from outside was killed. Meredith could see all of him clearly now.

Sarrett was holding a child, wrapped to the eyes in gray blankets.

The sight raised an unreasoning, savage frenzy in Meredith. "Put that brat down!" he yelled.

The boy that Sarrett unwrapped and stood on the dirt floor was pale and big-eyed, with a running nose and a face pinched from cold. He backed against Sarrett, staring at Meredith.

"Push him away," Meredith said.

"Shall I kick him across the room?" The boy had clutched Sarrett's leg.

Cattle bawled uneasily in the little valley while Meredith stood staring at Sarrett. This wasn't the man he had followed so long. It wasn't the insolent, laughing Sarrett who had ridden away from Gypsum Hill.

But still his name was Jack Sarrett and he had to die.

"How do I get this kid back where he belongs?" Meredith asked.

"He belongs here."

"You lie! Where's his folks? Where did you steal him?"

"His folks are dead," Sarrett said.

The Indian agency where Meredith had left his pack horse was only about thirty miles away. He could leave the kid there. "Your fingers warm enough?" he asked.

"Good enough . . . if I had a gun."

"You lie again! Unbutton that sheepskin."

Sarrett had no gun.

Everything was wrong with the way he'd planned things to go. "Your gun out there on your horse?"

"I've got a rifle behind the seat in the wagon."

Wagon? Meredith had heard no wagon. He studied Sarrett narrowly. "We'll get that gun," he said.

The boy hung tightly to Sarrett's hand as they walked through creaking snow to a spring wagon. It was going to be nasty for a kid, but when Sarrett tried his trick at the wagon. . . .

He didn't. First, he lifted from the box a calf that had been bedded down in sawdust. It bawled and ran to its mother tied behind the wagon. After a while Sarrett shoved the calf aside and stole some of the milk in a bucket.

Still ready with his gun, Meredith took the rifle. It had been put away so carelessly that Sarrett couldn't have got it out in a hurry if he'd tried.

For the first time since Sarrett kicked the door open, Meredith wasn't quite sure of how to handle things. They sat across the table from each other after the boy was asleep in the little bunk. Sarrett rolled a cigarette slowly. His hands were work-marked, Meredith observed. He'd be slow when the showdown came, so Meredith would have to see that he got an even chance.

It had to be settled Meredith's way. He'd ridden too far too many years for it to be any other way.

When the cigarette was going, Sarrett said: "I ran out on you down there at Elfego's place, sure. You weren't the first or last, but that's all set and done now."

"Almost." Meredith nodded. "Let's hear your side . . . if you've got one."

"No side to it," Sarrett said. "But I'll tell you if you'll hold off and listen."

The far valleys and towns flowed down his voice. The facts were all in and Sarrett denied none of them. He made some of them more damning. But from the first, Meredith sat looking at a man who didn't fit the past as it had been.

"Sure, I laughed about it all, and after you got on my tail and I found it out, I had more laughs from that than anything. It was a great . . . until I met a girl in Larned, Kansas." He looked up from under his brows. The candle was on a shelf above them, where Meredith had put it so it could not be knocked out quickly. It put deep hollows into Sarrett's face.

"I know, you've heard that one before, Brett. After you dropped a horn for me, you probably never looked seriously at any woman. You could always take 'em or ride on by, and so could I . . . until this happened."

Creaking cold put its weight against the cabin. The boy in the bunk breathed softly.

"She wasn't pretty," Sarrett said, "but there was something in her eyes and the way she smiled. . . ."

"Skip that part!"

"All right. She wouldn't marry me, and I know now, and should have known at the time, that it was a good thing she wouldn't . . . for her, at least. But I'll take an oath that I was honest and sincere at the time."

"Oh, sure!" Meredith said.

Sarrett stared at the table. "You know how it is when you've rolled out after the best night's sleep you ever had, and, while you're taking your first drag on a smoke, you look out on a range that's just been washed shining clean by rain, with the sky so clear it hurts to look at it . . . and you're not thinking about yourself at all, or any stunts you want to pull. For just a little while everything is like it ought to be with a man." Sarrett nodded to himself. "That's the way it was when I looked at Mary Linford."

"Damn you, I said to skip that stuff!" Mary's face was so clear that all Meredith's old hurt and bitterness came back. He saw Sarrett gave him a quick, odd glance.

"I don't say she changed me," Sarrett said. "I tried to change some and maybe I did . . . for a while. I know my thinking changed some." Shadows from outside and inside lay strongly on his face. "She was in love with a townsman, a two-by-four kid that had never been out in the rain. She finally made me believe it.

"I rode away, and I wasn't much good for a while. I pulled a few jobs and didn't get any kick out of them. The money went like it always did . . . with less pleasure I started back to see old Andy McRae in Texas, and that was a bad mistake. The Rangers got me cold. A bullet through the chest, three years in a cell. I won't say that I thought about my sins much, because all I thought about was busting out of there.

"When they let me go, I wasn't exactly the same man that went in, not that I wasn't glad enough to get out. I spent a week with Andy. They come and go at his place, so he knew you'd been after me." Sarrett looked up quickly. "He got the money you sent, Brett. Andy said to look you up and make peace. Believe me, or go to hell . . . that's what I started out to do when I left there."

"To hell with you."

"I stopped in Larned to see Mary. She was married, of course, and gone. I found her in Denver. Her husband had sunk his money in a mine that was nothing, and then he'd blown what little she had from her father. He couldn't stand being broke, and she was a drag to him then, so he

51

skipped out and went back to the hills."

Meredith clamped his jaw hard to keep from yelling a curse.

Sarrett's eyes were cloudy in the shadow-jumpy light. "She was working in a dance hall, Brett, one a little worse than most. It was the dirtiest jolt I've ever had to take to see her there. She wouldn't leave. I couldn't force her out. I offered her money and she said no. I didn't have it, but if she'd said yes, I'd have got it quick. She said she was going to save her money and hunt her husband up. He'd just had a little hard luck, she said."

Meredith leaned forward, his jaw muscles quivering, his face as stiff as brittle leather.

"I went looking for that husband, Brett. I told him where she was and his townsman's scruples stuck out all over him in a second. All he could ask me was why didn't she go back to her father. I knocked him clear across a room, and then I pulled my gun to kill him. I put it on him, and, between me and that gun, Mary's face came up as clear as I see yours now. When I got back to Denver, Mary was dead of pneumonia."

"Dead?"

Sarrett nodded, his eyes haunted and old. "Her boy had been left in an old shack with a drunken woman to take care of him."

Meredith's head jerked toward the little bunk.

Sarrett nodded. "That's him. I had him with some decent folks there, but this spring I knew they were going back East. I want him, Brett. His father has lost all right to him, and his grandfather is too old to do much for him."

Meredith rose. "I'm going to kill Roger Hammond."

Sarrett stared at him. "I'd begun to guess that you'd loved Mary, too."

"I'm going to kill Hammond."

"Sit down, Brett. We still have our problem."

Meredith sat down slowly. That was so. No matter what, this man was still Jack Sarrett. It was hard now to believe that he was, but he was.

"This is going to be the greatest ranching country in the state someday," Sarrett said. "My idea was to steal that herd and make a start for the boy. It's no good that way. When I went to Denver, I only lied a little . . . about the fifteen steers I shot. All right, there's no herd, but the country's still here, and I've seen it in summer. One of us is going to hold down everything I've filed on and make a spread for that boy someday."

Meredith licked his lips. He had no anger left against Jack Sarrett, and he couldn't figure where it had gone, but still the thought that had driven him was grooved in his brain, without a will.

"I traded my gun for that wagon," Sarrett said. "But you always carried a spare gun in your blanket roll. The moon ought to be up now. It'll be bright as day out there on the snow. We'll go far enough from the cabin so we don't scare the boy. When he wakes up in the morning . . . the one who isn't here just rode away in the night, understand?"

Sarrett shook his head slowly. "It isn't my way, Brett, and I know you think I'm trying to run something past you with talk. I told you when I left McRae's, it was with the idea of making peace if you wanted it. You don't want it, and that's all right with me. If I tried to crawl, I wouldn't be fit to think I could have raised Mary's boy and given him the right ideas about things."

Sarrett looked across the table steadily. A trace of his old smile flashed in the dark beard, a softer smile with the old mockery gone. "Anytime you say the word, Brett."

Meredith looked at the work-stiffened hands. He looked to where candlelight fell dimly on the sleeping boy.

Sarrett himself had gone a long way toward bringing decision. There were others though, and their words spoken far down the long trails of yesterday were just coming through to Meredith. Old Andy McRae, Pearl in the dirty room in Granada, and Mary Linford, with her eyes and smile as clear and beautiful as the range Sarrett had described.

The gun in Meredith's hand was far heavier now than it had been when he plunged and stumbled through the brush with fever swarming through him. He pushed it across the table.

Sarrett looked at it a moment. "I remember when you bought that in Austin. Mine was just like it." He pushed it back across the table.

Meredith picked it up and tossed it under the large bunk. He took off his hat, the fifth one that had carried the same small packet sewed inside.

"We got a hundred to start with," he said. "Two of us can do something with this country . . . and the boy."

The Luck of Riley

With a dab of dust in a buckskin poke Riley Winslow waited for the usual lecture before hitting the trail to Baker City.

Boone Adams wasn't old, but he was settled in his ways. He hunched his neck against his shoulder to squash a mosquito. He cleared his throat and said: "Luck is a grasshopper, Riley. A man jumps where it was while it's hopping somewhere else. Wait for it in one place, I say."

"I always come back in the fall, don't I? This time I got a feeling, Boone, an awful feeling. No telling what might happen." Riley grinned. "Anything special you want?"

Boone Adams gave the question deep consideration, looking toward the Poor Boy tunnel where a rickety wheelbarrow was ready to fall sidewise. He looked at a patched bellows hung under a tree near the portal of the tunnel. It leaked, it whistled, and sometimes it did not deliver enough air to the forge to keep a fire going.

"Nothing special, I guess," Boone said. "Just remember what I said about luck."

"I might even get back before fall."

Riley swung away, a slender man with bright blue eyes and a hunch that this summer luck was with him. Last year's dead leaves were floating away on the rise of Spikebuck Creek. The aspen leaves were small pale green. There was a feeling of a newness in the world.

In the Gulch Saloon Sam Tully hefted the dust with an expert's touch. "Seventy bucks, Riley. Considering you boys got only a knife-edge streak and have to grind your ore like an Indian making meal on a flat rock, and then pan it, I'd say you was doing fair. Streak ever going to widen out?"

"Boone says it will." Riley kept eyeing the poker game. It didn't look very tough.

"Boone's the hopeful kind, sure enough," Tully said. "How much do you want to leave behind the bar this time?"

"All but ten bucks."

Tully stacked ten silver dollars on the bar. "I hear there's a freighter over in Sweetwater that wants to sell a tramcar, some track, and a lot of stuff he hauled out from Denver for a fly-by-night mining outfit that flew. That stuff would be real handy at the Poor Boy."

"Awful handy," Riley said, "if a man had a thousand dollars to buy it."

He headed toward the poker table. In no time he knew that he and luck had jumped into the same chair. At dawn he had five hundred dollars and three placer claims in Lincoln Camp, the latter won on a beautiful little straight that beat three aces. The claims didn't count because anybody knew that Lincoln Camp, on the Little Beaver, was only a flash in the pan that wouldn't last till winter. But, of course, it wouldn't hurt to have a look at the property on the way to Sweetwater. It was just possible that a man with five hundred dollars might be able to make a deal with the freighter who had all that mining equipment to sell.

By the time he had walked to Lincoln Camp, Riley was wondering how one sky could have held so much water. He found the miners of the camp probing three feet of wash for tents and other belongings. He stopped beside a man who was trying to unwind a suit of red underwear from a willow thicket.

"Can you tell me where the Jim Dandy claims are?"

"You own 'em?"

"Yep."

The miner scowled. "Then you should have been here last night to get drowned with the rest of us. Your claims are up on the hill to the west. They ain't no good, but neither is anything else here. However, in case you was damn' fool enough to stick around, you'd be where you wouldn't get washed out of bed every time it rains."

Riley was not figuring to stick around, and he could see that no one else was either. He didn't go near his claims. By the time he had boiled a pot of coffee the few dozen miners of the gulch were stringing out toward Baker City. Riley would have thrown away his quitclaim deed to the Jim Dandy ground, but the paper was in the bottom of his pack. He headed for Sweetwater.

Where the trail broke over the wind-cold spine of Jingling Mountain, he met three Englishmen shivering beside a cairn. Their faces were gray and clammy from the altitude. Their pack horse had a list like the wheelbarrow at the Poor Boy mine.

"Lincoln Camp? Sure. I just came from there. Night before last a gully buster. . . ." Riley looked at the odd clothes of the Britons, at the ancient pack horse that somebody had unloaded on them.

The tallest man raised pale brows in a pained expression. "A gully buster? What in the world . . . ?"

"That means a rich strike," Riley said. "Yes, sir, things were really roaring in Lincoln Camp night before last."

"Ah, yes," one of the men said. "A reliable man in Saint Louis, Missouri, told us Lincoln Camp was one of the most prosperous . . . ah . . . diggings? . . . in America. I hope we're not too late."

"I'm afraid you are," Riley said. He saw disappointment shadow the faces of the Englishmen.

"You mean everything is taken?"

"The gulch was pretty well covered when I last saw it." Riley began to dig into his pack. "But it so happens that I own three claims down there. If it wasn't that my mother is very sick back in Maine. . . ."

He sold his claims for six hundred dollars. He went down the mountain singing, shying rocks at curious whistle-pigs.

The freighter in Sweetwater had the prettiest pile of mining equipment Riley had ever seen. Boone Adams would sit up all night talking when he saw all that stuff at the Poor Boy mine.

"Nine hundred for the works," the freighter said, "including the forge and ten sacks of blacksmith's coal. That just covers my expenses from Denver. All I want to do is get even."

"Four hundred," Riley said. "And fifty for your expenses from Denver. I'd like to keep you even, too."

The freighter spat against the pastern of a gray wheeler. "I can get a thousand any day by hauling the stuff over the hill to Lincoln Camp. Seven hundred where she lays. If I don't get that I'll go to Lincoln with the whole works."

"On second thought, four hundred is all I can stand," Riley said. "I have to work for my money. I don't own a rich claim like those fellows in Lincoln Camp."

"Six fifty?" the freighter asked.

Riley shook his head.

"Hell, I'm not giving things away. I'll head for Lincoln in the morning."

And that was what the freighter did. Sometimes, Riley thought, you have to make the grasshopper jump and then be waiting where he lands. The freighter could get over Jingling Mountain with his six-horse team, but it would take all his horses to bring an empty wagon up the west side, so there was going to be a fine bargain in mining equipment at Lincoln Camp.

Like any mushroom settlement, Sweetwater straddled the creek, spurning a fine level mesa fed by big springs just a quarter of a mile toward the southern spur of the main range. *There* was the place for the town that would spring here in earnest when someone got around to bringing in a railroad. The man who lived in a little cottonwood cabin on the mesa spent his time in Sweetwater, unloading wagons for two dollars a day.

"Sure I own the mesa," he told Riley. "Proved up on it last year." Three hundred dollars wasn't enough, he said. He ought to have fifteen hundred anyway.

Riley finally gave him five hundred, and within the hour had a surveyor laying out a town site. That night as he was automatically winning a few hundred bucks in a poker game, riders came down Puerta Pass with news that the Utes were cutting up again in the San Luis Valley on the other side of the main range. The riders said things were really fierce this time.

The poker players agreed that it was hard to make an honest living, what with the Indians always raising hell. A bushy-bearded little man said: "The Army ought to show them Utes how the boar et the cabbage."

"Them soldiers!" another man said. "In the first place, they won't come till we're all scalped . . . but if they do show up, it'll be like the last time when they tried to get through Puerta with wagons and got all tangled up like blind dogs in a smokehouse." He looked at his cards after the draw. "Bet twenty bucks."

Riley raised him, and then looked at his cards.

"If they'd leave their damned supply wagons behind and ride after the Indians, they might get something done," the bushy-bearded man said. He tossed in his hand.

Riley won the pot with a flush he had filled by drawing two cards. He raked in the chips absently.

The next day he bought a hammer-headed mule and rode up to have a look at Puerta Pass. Nature had left an easy grade, and travois had left the engineer's stakes. The Mormons would have considered the route a first-class pike, but everyone in Sweetwater had assured Riley that only a few wagons had ever worked all the way across. He guessed some people just didn't know luck when they saw it.

Before he left for Denver, he hired four teams and ten men to clear out the worst obstacles on Puerta. In three days the long-striding mule took him to Denver, and there he found the territorial legislature in session in a bar. For five dollars and two rounds of drinks the legislators gave him a franchise to operate a toll road on Puerta Pass. He spent one night playing poker and came to the conclusion that Denver poker players were the poorest in the world. Winning was getting sort of monotonous.

When he got back to Sweetwater, there was a road of sorts up the pass. Riley was smoking a good cigar and waiting at the tollgate when the Army came up the pass ten days later.

"What the hell is this?" a broad-beamed colonel on a black horse wanted to know.

"One dollar per horse, three dollars per wagon," Riley said, puffing a fine white cloud of smoke.

The colonel gave the impression of drawing his saber. "Have that gate opened at once!" he ordered a lieutenant, who twisted around to look at a sergeant who was already picking troopers for the job.

"Force that gate," Riley said, "and you'll prove to yourself that eagles have wings, Colonel. This toll road was built by private means, with the blessing of the government of the great Territory of Colorado under powers granted by the government of the United States of America, which in turn derives its authority. . . ."

"My God, a lawyer!" the colonel groaned. He cursed for quite a spell, and his face showed that government was no more comprehensible to him than to anyone else. But in the end he signed for a hundred men and twenty wagons, and all the while he kept giving Riley a dark court-martial stare. "What were you during the war?"

"Infantry private, C.S.A." Riley grinned. "Have a cigar, Colonel."

"I'll be damned." The colonel took the cigar and rode away.

Three days later the cavalry was back again, the colonel having learned that the Utes he sought were now in the Upper Arkansas Valley. Four days later they were over the hill again, and the colonel came back up the road with his command. By then Riley had a tent and a case of good whiskey. The colonel had a drink.

Troopers came and went. Army wagons came and went. The Army seemed to be supplying the cavalry in two places at the same time. Riley's hip pockets began to bulge with papers signed by the colonel. Between times he fished and drank whiskey and felt a little ashamed when he thought of

61

Boone Adams all alone at the Poor Boy with the leaky bellows and the Joe McGee wheelbarrow.

And then one day the colonel came down the pass with all his command. "Some fool went and made peace with the Utes before we could catch up with them," he said.

Riley shook hands with him and gave him three bottles of whiskey. He was going to miss the colonel. Travelers were now using the road in increasing numbers but collecting a miserable thirty or forty dollars a day began to bore Riley. Then, too, there were some people who always claimed they were going to a funeral, which gave them the right to use the toll road without charge. Riley didn't like to argue about such a solemn point, even when one man used the excuse six times.

One day Riley went to the owner of the biggest saloon in Sweetwater. "The toll road is a good thing," he said. "Someday the railroad will come this way, and that's the only good route over the range. They'll have to buy it. I'd wait till then . . . but I'm fed up with the country, and my mother back in Maine is awful sick, so for a measly ten thousand dollars. . . ."

"I'm pretty well fed up myself," the saloon man said, "although my mother lives in Tennessee." He shook his head sadly. "You can't tell about railroads, Riley. Railroads are funny things. I remember a town down in Texas where we expected the railroad to hit, and. . . ."

They settled on four thousand dollars. A party of dudes who fancied themselves as poker players hit town that night, and Riley won two thousand more, so he knew he still had the grasshopper pinned down.

A horse trader told him that a man of his ability should not be caught dead riding a hammer-headed mule, but Riley was fond of old Hammerhead by now, for the mule had bitten him only once and managed to kick him only twice, so he turned down all offers to trade and rode Hammerhead into Denver a second time.

"A few hours later, and you wouldn't have caught me in town," a high official of the War Department told Riley. "I can authorize prompt settlement of your toll-road charges. You're a lucky man, Mister Winslow. If you hadn't caught me, it might have taken months, more likely years . . . but, as it is. . . ."

"I jump with the grasshopper," Riley said.

After a few days he was doubly sure that Denver poker players were the world's worst. And then he had a fling at roulette in the Elephant Casino and broke the bank. He bought the place for twenty-five thousand dollars, attracted to it irresistibly because the checks were inlaid with beautiful blue grasshoppers.

For almost a month people waited five-deep to put their money on the tables in the renamed Grasshopper Casino. During that time the government paid off Riley's toll-road charges. He rode high. Everything he touched became money. He considered buying into a bank. And then one night a swamper, filling lamps, set fire to a five-gallon can of coal oil. The Grasshopper Casino made a hot, brisk fire, and a Kansan watching it go said that a place with a name like that ought to burn, by cracky.

Everybody got out with his life and it seemed that everybody also got out with pockets full of checks, most of which Riley knew full well had come from racks abandoned by cashiers. But he paid off, and he still had several thousand dollars left. The next day a government official presented him with a letter that said he had been overpaid nine hundred dollars on the toll road.

"It's best to settle now," the man said. "It might take the

government months, or even years, to collect if you contest the matter, but someday they will collect. It's better to adjust the matter now, don't you agree?"

Riley agreed and adjusted.

He sold the lots where his casino had stood and went up the street to tangle with the world's poorest poker players. They had learned something from watching him, he decided, when he went broke three hours later. He kept feeling his pockets. He couldn't believe it. He was actually broke.

A dumpy little man with ragged red whiskers approached him timidly and asked if he owned the mesa south of where Sweetwater used to be.

"What d'you mean . . . used to be?"

"Somebody made a big strike farther west. There's no one left at all on the creek." The man blinked apologetically, and his whiskers twitched with his words. "I've always had a hankering to start a little cattle ranch, so I thought. . . ."

"That's exactly what I had in mind for that mesa myself," Riley said. "Last week I almost bought the cows, but then I got word that my mother back in Maine is very sick, so for a thousand dollars, say. . . ."

"Oh, my!" the little man said. "That's way out of my class. I was hoping for a reasonable price."

Riley settled for three hundred dollars and a sturdy gray horse. For fifty dollars he sold to a gambling house the sack of inlaid checks, all but a pocketful of yellow ones with the beautiful blue grasshoppers in the center. These he kept for luck.

The wheelbarrow cost him fifty bucks. It did not have a steel bed, and it was more suitable for light gardening than mining, but still it was better than the one at the Poor Boy.

He bought, too, a brand new bellows for the forge. The sturdy gray pack horse carried both items easily, until fifteen miles from Denver the animal developed something that looked to Riley like a wonderful case of the blind staggers. Riley camped at once, picketing the horse to the wheel of the barrow. The gray appeared to recover, and it showed no concern at all over the fact that it was due for a quick trade.

Old Hammerhead's squeals woke Riley in the night. By the light of a low moon Riley fired three shots at figures scooting along on swift ponies. And by the light of the same moon he saw the wheelbarrow bouncing across the stony ground on the end of the picket rope tied to the gray, and the gray wasn't staggering a bit at the moment.

The Indians cut the rope, but not quite soon enough. At dawn Riley trailed down fragments of the wheelbarrow. There was nothing worth picking up. He flipped a yellow check at the wreckage and hoped that when the gray staggered its last stagger, it would fall smack on an Indian horse thief of any tribe or any description.

Grasshoppers were jumping everywhere in the fall-crisp grass when he rode into the valley of the Sweetwater. He met a railroad survey crew and asked the chief-of-party: "Where to?"

"First to Sweetwater," the chief said. "That'll be the division point, and then we'll run her up the old toll-road grade on Puerta."

"*Old* toll-road grade? Hell, that road's barely a pup," Riley said.

"It's old now," the chief said. "The railroad bought it from a saloon man for fifty thousand dollars."

"Is that a fact?" Riley rode up the valley with the bellows behind the saddle. He flipped yellow checks with grasshopper inlays at real grasshoppers.

Sweetwater had moved, sure enough. It was now up on the mesa, and it was a booming place. A timid little red-whiskered man was watching carpenters building a hotel. "How's your sick mother back in Maine?" he asked Riley.

"Much better. How's the cattle business?"

The man pointed at two milch cows browsing along the edge of the street. Riley bought the drinks.

"There was a flood on the creek," the little man said. "The saloons moved up here, and after that the rest of the town just naturally followed. You had a pretty good town site laid out here, Mister Winslow."

"I have an eye for such things," Riley said. He fixed a stern look on the little fellow. "While you didn't actually lie about the town moving, you did give me the impression that everybody had moved on to a strike in the mountains."

"Oh, there's a strike all right, a rich one on the Little Beaver. Lincoln Camp, where there used to be some placer workings, I understand."

Riley stayed one night in Sweetwater, playing poker. He couldn't win for losing. During the night somebody stole the bellows. He looked all over town, but he couldn't find it. He went on to Lincoln Camp.

The place was swarming. A miner told him three Englishmen had made the strike. "They didn't know nothing. They made a blind buy on the Jim Dandy claims from a man they met on top of Jingling Mountain. The claims weren't even in the gulch. They were on a hill. It so happened there had been a flood here that ran everyone out of camp. It also uncovered a rich vein of gold on the ground the Englishmen bought. They've had an offer of a hundred thousand dollars already."

"Bless me," Riley murmured, and bought the drinks.

"Them Englishmen had horseshoes in their pockets," the miner went on. "They no sooner were here than some freighter got lost and blundered down the mountain with the finest lay-out of mining equipment you ever seen. They bought the whole works, except the forge. It's the kind with a blower on it, a regular jim-dandy."

Riley winced at the description. "Who's got the forge?"

"The freighter went into business with it. He gets two bits a head for sharpening steel."

Under a lean-to in the trees the freighter was a busy man. He recognized Riley at once.

"How much for the forge, blower and all?" Riley asked.

"I'd sell you a claim on the hill for five thousand, not more'n half a mile from where the Englishmen made the strike, I'll swap horses or trade boots, but this here forge is a money-maker I can't part with."

"I passed two wagonloads of them on the way up here," Riley said. "How much for the forge?"

"It's worth five hundred, but I'll take four."

"Two hundred."

"Three hundred and the saddle on that mule."

The saddle was Riley's pride, but he had to take something back to Boone Adams. "If I throw in the saddle, how will the mule pack the forge?"

"For fifteen bucks I'll give you a packsaddle."

"Make it ten," said Riley.

After a half hour Riley knew that Hammerhead was not going to have anything to do with a packsaddle.

"I used to own that mule," the freighter said. "Never could make him wear a packsaddle. I'll tell you what I'll do . . . trade you straight across for that little sorrel over there. She's a great pack horse."

The little sorrel had one hip high in the air and the other

braced against a tree. "What happens if you move that aspen?" Riley asked.

"When she packs, she packs," the freighter said. "When she rests, she rests. She's a jim-dandy on the trail."

"I'm tired of that word," Riley said.

When Hammerhead saw what was happening, a bitter, ornery expression came into the mule's eyes. It hurt Riley to part with Hammerhead, but he had to take the forge back to Boone, so he made the deal.

The sorrel was a packer sure enough; she went right along until, at the top of a rocky pitch a few miles from Baker City, Riley stopped to light his pipe. It was a large grasshopper lighting on the sorrel's cheek that started all the trouble. She knocked Riley flat and went bucking down the hill. The packsaddle slipped, and the forge came dangling down the side.

Riley found fragments of cast iron for a mile before he caught up with the mare tangled up in the trees. Even the packsaddle wasn't much good then, so he cut it loose and went on into Baker City.

Sam Tully said: "You're back a little earlier than usual this year. Have a good summer?"

"One of the best," Riley said, and bought the drinks.

It was not long afterward that Hammerhead clattered up the street, dragging a broken halter rope, and then the freighter who owned him arrived a little later.

"You spoiled that mule," the freighter said. "He pried up hell, kicking and biting all my horses, and then he busted loose."

"I forgot to tell you," Riley said, "when he raises hell, he bites and kicks. I'll tell you what I'll do . . . I'll trade the sorrel back for the mule."

The freighter spat and bought the drinks. "I got to have

something for my trip down here."

"You can have the packsaddle."

"I saw it. Give me the sorrel and thirty bucks to boot, and you can have the hammerhead back."

"Make it fifteen." Forty dollars was all Riley had.

"Thirty. And I'll throw in the halter on the mule. That's my figure." The freighter stood so firmly on the point that Riley finally had to pay.

When the freighter was gone and Hammerhead was leering through the window with a triumphant smirk, Sam Tully said: "Boone done drew all the dust you left behind the bar."

Riley said: "He always was a spendthrift."

When a poker game started that afternoon, Riley jumped in with his ten bucks. He lost it in one hand, having a miserable little straight beaten by a flush.

Golden aspen leaves were floating on Spikebuck Creek when he rode bareback up the mountain, singing a song to the mule.

"Well, you're back," Boone Adams said. He was glad to see Riley, but at the moment he was busy tinkering with the wobbly wheelbarrow. There were a few more patches on the bellows above the stone forge, and a good deal more rock over the dump. "Looks like you had a lucky summer, Riley. That's a stout-looking mule you got there."

"It was a good summer." Riley had one yellow chip left. He spun it through the air to his partner. "Would you believe that was once worth a hundred dollars?"

Boone examined the check curiously.

"Streak widen any?" Riley asked.

"Not yet, but it will," Boone said absently. "That's a good-looking chip, Riley. It reminds me of something. Luck is a grasshopper. A man jumps. . . ."

"You could be right," Riley said.

A Trap for Chicken Bill

As anyone can plainly see, and Deputy Sheriff Thomas Jefferson McCrumb could see most plainly down the barrel of his rifle, this Chicken Bill was a bad one—much worse than McCrumb had expected.

His jaw was long and sharp. His mean little eyes crowded the bridge of his thin nose. They were busy at the moment with peering all around the opening in the laurel thicket. He wore a better hat than any thief had a right to wear, and his foxy little ears were listening for the merest sound.

In his left hand was a rifle, which McCrumb judged was somewhat better than his own. In his right was a sack. Up here on the Cheat River, folks set great store by their chickens, and so apparently did Chicken Bill, for the sack wiggled now and then and gave out muffled squawks.

McCrumb thought he might be just a few rods over the county line, but that was of no great importance; what mattered was that he must get a mite closer to the opening in order to capture Chicken Bill without shooting him. Folks in Schenley County liked to see the law upheld, particularly against other folks, but they would laugh McCrumb right out of the race he had intended to make for sheriff if he had to wound a hen house thief to bring him in, even a desperate, notorious thief like Chicken Bill.

The more he looked at Chicken Bill, the surer McCrumb was that people would appreciate how dangerous a task this had been, once they saw Chicken Bill in jail.

Easing forward in a crouch, McCrumb tried to get a little closer to the opening. A branch bent against his shoulder, and before he could catch it there came a tiny *swishing* noise. He heard his man jump. McCrumb leaped up with his rifle ready.

"Halt there!"

McCrumb was talking to space. Chicken Bill had already dived to cover. If McCrumb had a conscience about shooting a thief, Chicken Bill had none about shooting a deputy sheriff. He fired. His bullet seared almighty close to McCrumb, who fell flat on the ground and replied in a natural manner. The laurel rang to merry sounds for several moments. Then, making a flank sneak, McCrumb began to suspect what he would find: nothing. He was right. Chicken Bill had made a fool of another deputy sheriff.

"He's tricky as an old razorback," Sheriff Bert Adams had warned McCrumb. "When folks get red hot in Schenley County, he moves over the ridge and works Perry County for a spell. I've heard say he sometimes hangs around Old Man Brown's place. You might run into him there, but I don't know." Sheriff Adams had clasped his hands on his stomach.

"What about this Old Man Brown?"

"Not him. His daughter. She's a fine looker. Deputies chasing Chicken Bill have been known to hang around Old Man Brown's place so much they forgot what they went up there after."

McCrumb had grunted. "I'll have him inside a week."

With a little luck it would have been two days.

McCrumb heard a squawk in the opening. By Ned, he had done one thing at least: he had scared Bill loose from his loot. There were four hens in the sack, nice fat ones. Just for an instant McCrumb understood why a man would steal chickens. He hefted the bag, looking at the sun.

It was too late now to go tramping after Chicken Bill. The next move was to head for Old Man Brown's. A fine looker, his daughter. McCrumb wondered about that. Some of those lop-eared deputies from Perry County might think so, but Thomas Jefferson McCrumb came from a settlement with a regular population of a hundred and fifty people. No bare-footed ridge-runner girl would blind him to duty.

He came at sunset to the cabin that sat on a hill with a fine grove of oaks behind it. The garden plot was fenced; spring water ran through one side of the yard; chickens were busy in the weeds, and a dozen hogs went wallowing off into the brush when they saw McCrumb.

The girl came to the edge of the porch and stood there in the sunset looking at him. Her hair was red gold. She gave McCrumb a slow, white-toothed smile that spoke of impudence—and other things. She was straight and tall, and her dress was not the loose flour sack that he had expected to see. It fit her snugly, and it occurred to Deputy McCrumb that a dozen yards of calico might be as necessary to dressing up as he had thought.

Her legs were brown, and her feet were brown . . . and bare. *What was wrong with bare feet?* he asked himself. He had gone that way until he was sixteen and moved to the settlement. He took the sack of chickens from his shoulder.

"I'm Deputy Sheriff Thomas Jefferson McCrumb."

"Howdy."

There was a world of welcome in her slow greeting.

"Your pa around, Miss Brown?"

"Caroline," she said in the same slow voice. "Pa's out berrying. I'm pleased to know you, Mister Deputy. Won't you set on the porch and I'll get you a drink. You look all hot and tired."

"Maybe I will. I been chasing Chicken Bill all over these hills. Mighty near had him, too, once."

"You did!"

"Sure as can be, only I didn't want to shoot him. I'm not a man to go shooting folks without warning." McCrumb sat down in a willow chair. The next time he got a bead on Chicken Bill, warning or no warning. . . .

"Wouldn't you rather sit in this chair, Mister Deputy?" Caroline asked. "That one's in Perry County, and since you're an officer from Schenley County. . . ."

"I'd be happy to." McCrumb moved. "The line runs smack through the house, huh?"

"Right through the middle." Caroline brought McCrumb a glass of water.

One thing, they sure had good water from these limestone springs.

He noticed that Caroline's dress was a dark plaid, good honest Scotch colors. Down in the settlement they would say it was a little short and too soon in places. But he liked it that way. Some of those old women down there were odd.

McCrumb cleared his throat. "Have you seen Chicken Bill lately?"

"Not for several days."

"He comes here sometimes, don't he?"

"Yes, he does."

You could tell she had no use for Chicken Bill.

"How come your pa don't run him off?"

She pointed at the chickens pecking weeds along the garden fence. "He might take offense and steal us blind."

McCrumb nodded. That was exactly what Chicken Bill would do to a lone girl and a helpless old man. The sack in the yard stirred, and one of the captives protested.

"Chickens," McCrumb said. "I shot the sack right out of his hands, but he leaped away like a weasel. Maybe you could tell me whose chickens they are."

With their heads close together they peered into the sack. McCrumb would have kept peering, but Caroline straightened up and stepped back a little. She said: "They look like Perry County chickens to me."

"That's what I thought." McCrumb frowned. "I can't be loading myself down with them, and I ain't got the time to search for the owner. The only thing left is to cook 'em."

Caroline gave a little gasp. Her eyes were smoky blue. "Would that be lawful like?"

McCrumb nodded judiciously. "If I left 'em here alive, the owner might come along sometime when I was gone and say you was aiding and abetting Chicken Bill. When the owner of the evidence can't be found, the best thing to do is use the evidence for the benefit of the county. Since you might invite me to stay here. . . ."

"Oh, I'm sure Pa will, Mister Deputy."

"Tom."

He helped Caroline dress the four hens on a plank table near the kitchen door.

"It must be terribly lonely up here . . . for a pretty girl."

"There's Pa and me," Caroline said vaguely. McCrumb could see how lonely she was. "And Willie Dabney. He drops by sometimes. Oh, there's folks around."

She was pining away. A pretty girl like that up here in the hills. She deserved much better; something, say, like walking down the street in Brantley on the arm of Deputy Thomas Jefferson McCrumb.

"Who's Willie Dabney?" McCrumb asked.

"He's a friend. We grew up together. Pa sort of likes him, and I guess he's always figured that Willie and me. . . ." Caroline made a vague gesture with the knife above the chickens. "Well, you know. . . ." She blushed.

"You deserve something better than this!" McCrumb said. He looked around. Some of the hogs he had scared away were poking their snouts out of the oaks, grunting with suspicion.

They finished the chickens. Caroline took them inside, and McCrumb sat down on the porch. It might, after all, take about a week to catch Chicken Bill. During that time McCrumb's bounden duty also included convincing Caroline that this was no place for a girl like her.

The sheriff's job paid ten dollars more a month. There was that little house that Amos Hornaday wanted to rent, and it was just right for a young couple. . . .

The sound of frying chicken came from the house. *Gosh, she was a pretty girl.* McCrumb sat on the porch in a pleasant fog, figuring and figuring.

It sounded like a footstep somewhere behind the house. McCrumb came out of his daze and went along the porch with his rifle ready. Maybe Caroline's pa was coming back, but you just couldn't take any chances. He went around the corner of the house and looked in the back yard. The hogs had eased a little closer. That was it. . . . It must have been the hogs.

McCrumb went back to the porch. Just stepping up on the other end of it was Chicken Bill.

They put their rifles on each other.

"Drop your rifle," Chicken Bill snarled.

"Drop yours."

"I gotcha!"

Deputy McCrumb considered a moment. "I got you . . . you mean!"

For a while it looked like a stalemate.

From about where the gate would have been, if there had been a fence across the front yard, a deep voice caused both Chicken Bill and McCrumb to jump.

"Both of you put down them rifles!"

There stood a little pink-faced man with one of the biggest fowling pieces McCrumb had ever seen. As a minor point of interest, a pail heaped with blackberries was near his feet.

"I ain't having no feuding around my place. Put them guns down, you two."

McCrumb and Chicken Bill looked at each other. They obliged.

"Trouble, trouble," Old Man Brown said. He came forward briskly, a beady-eyed little rooster hardly big enough to handle the two-barreled fowling piece, but he was handling it.

With one eye on Chicken Bill, McCrumb decided to be content for a while.

From the doorway Caroline said: "Supper in a few minutes, Pa."

"You boys is welcome to eat with us and stay the night," Old Man Brown said, "but I want them rifle guns left out in the woods whenever you're around here. Hear me?"

Chicken Bill nodded reluctantly.

"That's fair." McCrumb was in the wrong county now. When he went around the porch to his side of the line,

Chicken Bill made a careful sashay down the porch to the Perry County side. A fat lot of good that would do him the first time McCrumb caught him a hundred yards from Old Man Brown's.

Picking up the rifles, Old Man Brown examined them with interest, making little clucking noises all the time. He went around the house and was gone for several minutes. Chicken Bill began to lower himself into a chair. McCrumb sat down at the same speed. They eyed each other. Chicken Bill was undoubtedly the evilest-looking thing ever let loose in the hills, McCrumb was sure.

He heard Caroline and her pa talking in low tones. The poor girl must be nervous as all get-out over having Chicken Bill and an officer around at the same time.

"You ain't staying for supper," McCrumb said. "Not even should they insist out of kindness."

"Ain't I?"

"No!" McCrumb stood up.

Chicken Bill stood up.

Old Man Brown stepped through the doorway, his fowling piece across one skinny arm. "Trouble, trouble. By Harry, are you going to be decent, or do I run both of you off?"

Chicken Bill and McCrumb sat down again.

Caroline said: "Supper's ready."

"You're a mighty eater," Old Man Brown said to Chicken Bill halfway through the meal.

A mighty hog, McCrumb thought. He was keeping up with Chicken Bill only out of politeness to Caroline's good cooking.

Out in the dusk there came the sound of a banjo and someone singing "Roll Away".

"That's Willie!" Caroline said. She went out, and

McCrumb heard her talking to Willie Dabney.

They came inside a few moments later. One glance told McCrumb that Willie was no real problem, even with a banjo. He was a shy-looking specimen with fine curly hair, with his jeans all faded pale blue. Why, he was hardly old enough to be looking at girls, the big, bare-footed gawk.

"You et, Willie?" Old Man Brown asked.

"Uh . . . well, I guess I did. A little." Willie eyed the chicken.

"Set down," Old Man Brown said.

Willie's appetite was mighty, too. In self-defense, McCrumb stayed with him; and Chicken Bill—well, he was a hog by nature. And so, directly there were no chickens left.

Willie leaned back in his chair. "So you finally killed those four lazy hens, huh, Caroline?"

"Why . . . ," Caroline said.

"They never laid enough to earn their keep," Old Man Brown said.

Chicken Bill eyed McCrumb, and McCrumb glared right back at him.

"Let's set on the porch while Caroline's redding up the kitchen," Old Man Brown said. "Will, you can play us a tune or two."

"Why, I'd be pleasured to," Will said.

Will was a fair banjo player, McCrumb thought, but, of course, it didn't take any brains for that. Out in the dark the hogs settled down, squealing and grunting a little. The chickens murmured sleepily, roosting here and there on the buildings. A cool breeze ran out of the grove of oaks.

McCrumb and Chicken Bill glowered at each other through the spill of lamplight from the house, and then they sat down again.

"I swear there ain't been a real brisk rain since May," Old Man Brown said, as if he had a hundred acres under crops.

"Play 'Hogs in the Cornfield', Will," Caroline said.

Will played and sang. He didn't have a voice for sour apples, McCrumb thought, although he did stay on the tune, as near as McCrumb could tell. Old Man Brown hummed, like a bullfrog with a mouth full of mosquitoes. Then Will played and sang "Sweet Amantha".

Chicken Bill said: "Do you know 'Dublin City', Dabney?"

"I don't guess I do, by that name. How does it go?"

Chicken Bill hummed a tune. McCrumb sniffed.

"No, I don't know that one, I guess," Will said.

"Mind if I try your banjo?" Chicken Bill asked.

"I'd be pleasured to have you try it."

After a while McCrumb had to allow that Chicken Bill's voice was fair. In some ways he was about as good as Will on the banjo, not that it meant anything.

"Why, that was real pretty!" Caroline said.

The note of admiration got under McCrumb's hide. "I've heard better."

Chicken Bill sang a half dozen songs. Caroline and Will liked them all. McCrumb tried to tell about a shooting match he had seen over on the Piney, but no one was interested. Old Man Brown did say: "Is that a fact?" And then he asked Chicken Bill to play another song.

All of a sudden Chicken Bill got up and handed the banjo to McCrumb. "Wouldn't you like to play us a tune?"

"I never had no time for that foolishness." Full of rage and frustration, McCrumb gave the instrument back to Will.

Old Man Brown yawned. "Not a drop of rain . . . so help

me. You two fellers can sleep in the barn, if you promise fair not to do any gouging and fighting."

Chicken Bill and McCrumb promised. The barn was in Schenley County. When the two guests climbed into the hayloft, McCrumb considered kicking Chicken Bill down the ladder and then saying that he had fallen. Only one thing stopped him! Chicken Bill made McCrumb go clean to the far end of the loft before he came up the ladder.

After that McCrumb decided he'd just as well keep his promise to Old Man Brown. He heard Caroline talking to Willie Dabney in the yard, and then Willie went down the trail alone, playing his banjo.

Caroline was prettier than ever at breakfast. It fair took McCrumb's breath away to see a woman shining like that so early in the morning. Right after they ate, Old Man Brown took McCrumb and Chicken Bill outside.

"Your rifle gun is in the first crotch of that big burr oak above the spring," Old Man Brown told McCrumb. "And yours is leaning again' that catalpa over that way," he told Chicken Bill.

McCrumb hung back after Chicken Bill started. "I'll have him off your hands as soon as I can, Mister Brown. If he don't light clean out of the country, I may get him today."

"Trouble, trouble," the old man said.

Chicken Bill walked faster and faster, and then ran. McCrumb had to run, too.

Before the day was over it became apparent to McCrumb that his man was not intending to light clean out of the country. In fact, Chicken Bill showed no intention of going very far from Old Man Brown's place. In the middle of the morning McCrumb got a long-range shot that made

Chicken Bill leap fifteen feet to cover.

In the afternoon, when McCrumb was lunching on blackberries in a patch, Chicken Bill put a bullet through his hat. McCrumb had to crawl a hundred feet through stickers and over burned logs to reach the trees. He was in a fine rage when that was done.

Toward sundown he worked back to Old Man Brown's. From the edge of the burr oaks he surveyed the yard, wondering whether or not to leave his rifle. Of course he had promised, but. . . . He kept thinking of how he had been forced to wriggle away from the blackberry patch.

He guessed he'd go in with the rifle.

"Ah, ah!" a deep voice said, and there was skinny Old Man Brown sitting on a stump with his fowling piece.

McCrumb left his rifle. The first thing he noticed when he went in the house was the tremendous pan full of frying chicken. Caroline's face was flushed from the fire. She sure was pretty. She eased around to the other side of the stove when McCrumb might have put an arm around her.

"I didn't aim for you to kill any of your chickens just for me, Caroline."

"I didn't. These were left here in a sack today."

McCrumb ground his teeth. "How'd Chicken Bill sneak back here with me on his trail the whole day?" And then he wished he had kept still.

"He didn't sneak," Caroline said. "He walked in big as you please, left the chickens, and walked off again. I think they're Schenley County chickens, but when I got to remembering what you said about evidence. . . ."

Once more Chicken Bill made a hog of himself at supper. As a Schenley County officer dealing with property rightfully belonging in Schenley County, McCrumb was obliged to get his share.

McCrumb offered to help with the dishes. Chicken Bill told them both to sit on the porch and rest themselves. When Caroline came out, McCrumb said he hadn't tried to smoke an Indian "seegar" from a catalpa tree since he was a kid. He wondered if Caroline could show him where there was a catalpa all podded out.

Chicken Bill said he would like to go along, so nobody went any place. Willie Dabney came shuffling up the trail with his banjo. Again everybody sat on the porch and listened to Willie and Chicken Bill play the banjo and sing their mournful songs.

McCrumb thought he'd never seen such a stubborn pack of idiots. Anyone should have known that he and Caroline wanted to be alone.

When Chicken Bill and McCrumb went to the barn that night, it was Chicken Bill's turn to go up the ladder first. He made a clever pretense about going to the far end of the loft, and, if McCrumb had not been extra careful, he would have got kicked clean back to the barn floor when he stuck his head into the loft.

As it was, McCrumb ducked. Chicken Bill's big foot made a *swishing* sound when he missed, and then he cursed like a low-down thief, which he was, of course.

They settled down in opposite corners of the mow. It occurred to McCrumb that Schenley County folks would give him the horse laugh if they ever found out about him sleeping with a chicken thief he was sworn to catch. A little later, listening for any rustling sound that would indicate Chicken Bill was trying to creep over and strangle him, McCrumb developed a troublesome suspicion of Old Man Brown.

The next day when Chicken Bill and McCrumb

ducked into the woods to grab their rifles and take up the day's affairs, McCrumb made a big feint and came back to Old Man Brown's place, watching it from the edge of the trees.

Caroline's pa took his fowling piece and a bucket and went into the woods, and McCrumb trailed him all day long. In the afternoon McCrumb became so engrossed in watching Old Man Brown, who was acting mighty innocent near a cabin where chickens ranged all around, that he forgot Chicken Bill.

Chicken Bill did not forget anything. He clipped bushes all around McCrumb, and once more McCrumb was forced to make a belly crawl over some rough ground. That made it worse. At the end of it he almost bumped into Old Man Brown's legs. Caroline's pa was standing behind a tree. His pail was full of blackberries.

"Might' near' got you, didn't he?" Old Man Brown said. He clucked his tongue and started home with his blackberries.

There had been five chickens in the sack Chicken Bill left with Caroline that day. "That ugly brute!" McCrumb said. "And me watching him every second of the day, almost." He could hardly admit he had been suspicious of Caroline's innocent old pa.

"The chickens do help out," Caroline said. "What with all the extra mouths to feed."

She made McCrumb feel like a no-good who could not support a wife, even if he had one. The more he thought about it, the madder he got at Chicken Bill. The lantern-jawed sneak was trying to be smart, showing off in front of Caroline.

That night McCrumb decided he had heard enough banjo music to last a lifetime. While Chicken Bill was singing "Foggy Dew", McCrumb got Willie to walk down to the hog pen.

If folks sort of laughed at the law up here, they were still impressed by it, McCrumb knew. He assumed a stern manner. "Me being an officer of the county, I've got to know how Chicken Bill manages to steal hens right in broad daylight."

Willie shuffled his feet. "He's got a mean temper. If he thought you'd pumped anything from me. . . ."

"I'll protect you, Willie. It's your duty to tell me anything you know about Chicken Bill. How he steals chickens in broad daylight, that is."

"Well . . . ," Willie said. "I've heard say one way he gets hens in the daylight is like this. . . ."

The next day McCrumb lay in the bushes near the cabin where he had seen all the chickens. At intervals he flipped a few bits of cracked corn toward a dozen hens. They were shy; they did not trust the bushes. But gradually they let themselves be led toward the strings of corn that led to snares. One hen, more greedy than the rest, finally went up the corn trail in a hurry.

She tripped a snare and went up in the air with a frightened squawk, and then she began to flop and beat her wings. McCrumb had not realized that one hen could make so much racket. He crawled over to grab her.

Someone at the cabin howled: "Chicken Bill!"

McCrumb grabbed the hen and his rifle. A rifle cracked, a shotgun boomed. The way the shotgun cut the bushes it must have been loaded with bits of a broken kettle, McCrumb thought. He ran low and got away.

All that trouble for one miserable chicken. McCrumb raised up to have a look and get his bearings. He saw

Chicken Bill just in time to duck again. For the third time McCrumb had to crawl like a worm while bullets raked around him. Finally he crept up a little ridge, and then he made it hot for Chicken Bill.

A woman at the cabin yelled: "Don't go out there in the bresh, Lem! There's a dozen of them!"

Lem did not heed the advice. He almost flanked McCrumb. It must have been nuts and bolts in the shotgun this time. They whizzed around McCrumb and knocked chunks of rotten wood from the log that protected him.

"Oh, Lord," he muttered. From sleeping in the same barn with a chicken thief, he had gone to stealing hens himself. It probably would not look just right to Lem and the other man with the rifle. Of course, he could say he had taken the hen from Chicken Bill, almost catching the man in the act.

But then McCrumb decided Lem was not in the mood to listen that long. Thomas Jefferson McCrumb retreated hastily, still holding onto the chicken. He went back to Old Man Brown's; it seemed like the safest place.

Old Man Brown was watching the weeds grow in the garden. He looked at the chicken. "Scrawny," he said. "Caroline can't abide a scrawny chicken. Where'd you get it?"

"I shot it out of Bill's hands."

"Trouble, trouble. Why didn't you wait till he had some fat ones?"

McCrumb wished he had thrown the hen away back there in the woods. It was too late now. Caroline came to the door.

"I suppose Chicken Bill left another sack full of hens today," McCrumb said.

"Not today. You must have kept him too busy."

"You're right. I almost had him."

"That's a scrawny hen you got there."

Once more Caroline made McCrumb feel that he was so worthless, he couldn't even steal a decent hen.

When Willie showed up for supper that night even he had the courage to hint that collard greens and one small, thin chicken didn't make much of a meal. McCrumb told him to mind his manners, if he had any. Chicken Bill was surly. McCrumb could appreciate that. Even if the one hen wasn't much, it proved that McCrumb had beaten Chicken Bill at his own game.

Once was enough, considering Lem. The whole affair was getting dangerous. Tomorrow Chicken Bill was going to jail, if he had to go feet first. Truce or no truce, when McCrumb returned to Old Man Brown's tomorrow, he was coming in armed. The only thing that worried him was Caroline; she might get hurt.

Right after supper McCrumb went back into the kitchen for a drink of water. He told Caroline what he was going to do. She gave him a scared look.

"Don't worry about me," he said. "I'll be all right. I won't hurt your pa, either, but maybe it would be best if you could sort of keep him out of the way about dusk."

"I'll try," she said.

The way she looked at McCrumb made them partners, maybe even more. He went over to pat her shoulder and maybe slip his arm around her, but just then Chicken Bill came in, with suspicion all over his mean face.

"Go sing something pretty," McCrumb said.

"Yeah? I will if Miss Caroline says so."

There was a nice heavy poker in the wood box. McCrumb reached toward it. He'd just as well start taking Chicken Bill to jail right now.

"No! Please, no!" Caroline cried.

"Just no," Old Man Brown said, standing there with his two-barrel. "I'm getting downright tired of keeping peace." He cocked both barrels.

Chicken Bill and McCrumb went back to the porch. Willie was playing a lonesome little song, too dumb to know what had been going on inside. After a while Chicken Bill sang. The way he slobbered over love songs was enough to turn a man's stomach.

McCrumb tried, in between songs, to tell about a hunting trip with his cousin down in the balsams. But again no one showed much interest, except Willie, who didn't count.

All the next day Chicken Bill was sneakier than ever. McCrumb didn't get one fair shot at him, but, on the other hand, he didn't have to do any crawling himself. At dusk he came to the edge of the trees and studied the house. By now the hogs were getting used to him, and they made no fuss. He could hear Chicken Bill humming to himself in the kitchen.

McCrumb took off his shoes and went in against a blind angle of the house. He crept up to the kitchen door and leaped inside. He surprised Chicken Bill and Old Man Brown, but not quite enough.

Chicken Bill's rifle was pointing at the doorway, and McCrumb was in the doorway.

"Gotcha!" McCrumb said.

"I got you! Drop the gun!"

Old Man Brown sighed. "I guess the two of you got each other for fair this time. This sneak here . . ."—he looked sadly at Chicken Bill—"snuck up and disarmed me."

"Chicken Bill, I'm an officer of the law. Are you coming peaceful like, or . . . ?"

"*Me* come peaceful like! You mean *you'd* best come along. . . ." Chicken Bill's eyes squinted down to nothing. "Chicken Bill! Man, you been looking at the moon too much. I'm Deputy Sheriff Bolivar Martin Ames from Perry County."

"Huh!" McCrumb said. "I imagine. Put down. . . ."

"You're Chicken Bill yourself!"

"I'm Deputy Sheriff Thomas Jefferson McCrumb from Schenley. . . ."

"Yeah! I seen you trying to bait chickens into a snare."

"That's a lie!" McCrumb yelled. "The first day I was here I shot you loose from a sack of four fat hens. . . ."

"That's a lie! I almost had *you* that day, and then you crept in on my back, like you tried to do a minute ago!"

"Did you see me with the hens?" McCrumb demanded.

"Sure! I saw you running through the laurel, with a sack of squawking chickens. . . ."

"Me?"

"Someone."

All at once a lot of heat was gone from the room.

"Trouble, trouble," Old Man Brown muttered happily.

Certain damp fears crept in on McCrumb through every barrier he tried to erect. "Let's see your badge."

"Let's see yours."

The two men stared at badges taken from under their shirts. Old Man Brown craned to peer with interest. "I do believe the Perry County one is the prettiest."

"Something's wrong," McCrumb said in an ominous voice.

"It do seem so," Old Man Brown said.

They turned on him fiercely. "Where's Caroline?" McCrumb demanded.

"Visiting her cousins over in Maple County. We got lots

of kinfolks there. Every year about this time. . . ."

"Where's that Willie Dabney?"

"Oh, he traipsed along. He's got kin there, too, might' near' as many as Caroline and me."

McCrumb and Ames looked at each other.

"Chicken Bill," they said together sadly.

"Some folks do call Will that," Old Man Brown said.

"Aiding and abetting," McCrumb said. "Old Man Brown, you're going with me."

"With *me*," Ames said. "He's setting on the Perry County side of the kitchen. Aiding and. . . ."

"Who et the chickens?" Old Man Brown asked. "Right along with Chicken Bill."

McCrumb raised one foot and somewhat absently removed a splinter from it. "I reckon we'd best forget the aiding and abetting."

"Yeah," Ames said.

"You're right nice boys," Old Man Brown said. "So I'm going to tell you something. Far as I know, no sheriff ever did come up here looking for Chicken Bill. They always send their deputies. Now if you boys ever figure someday to run for sheriff, don't you let nobody send you up here. It just ruins a man's political chances."

McCrumb looked sidewise at Ames, and Ames returned the look in the same manner.

They walked across the road together, and then they parted quickly, glad to be out of each other's company.

Old Man Brown stood in the yard, looking at the sky. "Not a real brisk rain since May," he said. And then he began to laugh.

McCrumb was a hundred yards down the trail before he remembered that he was barefoot. He guessed he'd just leave it be.

"I'll Kill You Smiling, John Sevier"

They were bounty hunters, Frank Moxon and Dave Delaplane, men who took deputy sheriffs' commissions anywhere they could get them, then rode forth to collect reward money on the heads of wanted men.

Now they were in South Fork, after a man who had changed his name to John Sevier, who was worth two hundred and fifty dollars dead or alive in Kansas. It was not much, but Moxon said it would pay their expenses to Durango.

For ten years, Moxon had been a bounty hunter. He was well known, well hated, and he had been recognized at the livery at South Fork before he swung out of the saddle.

Delaplane was new to the business; he had done one job with Moxon. From the door of the livery Delaplane watched the old man who had recognized Moxon hurry to spread the news.

"I like people to know I'm around," Moxon said.

They were going down the street to the sheriff's office when a man carrying a boot came from the mercantile. He had been laughing, but then the humor was crushed out under a terrible awareness.

"Another one knows you," Delaplane said.

"He ought to." Moxon smiled. "That's the man I came to get, John Sevier."

Through the window of the sheriff's office, Delaplane caught a glimpse of a heavy-featured man sitting inside. Moxon said—"All right, Delaplane."—and went in.

Delaplane stood by the wall, at the side of the open doorway, watching the town. Things began to buzz.

The voice inside the sheriff's office was slow and heavy. "This warrant is sort of old, isn't it, Moxon?"

"Murder warrants don't run out."

The sheriff's voice was flat. "How come you're this far away from the big money?"

"A little here, a little there," Moxon said.

They sparred, the sheriff getting the worst of it. So far, the name of the wanted man had not been mentioned. Moxon would get to that in his own way.

Delaplane watched the town. Moxon had said Sevier was a man who had run once but who would not run again. Moxon was generally right about men.

To reach South Fork, he and Moxon had crossed two mountain ranges and then ridden through cattle and farming land. The town was on the edge of both. There seemed to be plenty of business.

About half the buildings were of stone or sand brick. Water ran in a small ditch at the edge of the flagged walk. Delaplane decided it was the air of permanence that gave the town its slow look and made it different.

The sheriff's voice had lost its calmness. He was saying: "When you lay that money on a bar, don't it bother you, Moxon? Don't you remember how you made it?"

"My way suits me," Moxon said. "If you don't understand me, I don't understand men like you who keep bragging what a peaceful village you've got. When I show up to help you keep it that way, you get edgy."

"This town doesn't need your kind of law, Moxon."

"Do you want to see my commission?"

"I know about you."

Moxon laughed quietly. The aroma of his cigar drifted out to Delaplane. It was a fifty-center, and, because of what the sheriff said, Deplane remembered how Moxon had spilled silver on a bar to buy a handful of them. The bartender had not used tongs to pick it up.

Moxon got to his point. "Is John Westrum here?"

"I don't know anyone by that name."

"Do you know him by the description on the dodger?"

"No."

"Do you want to look again, Sheriff? It's ten years old. I don't look like I did ten years ago. Would you say you do?" Moxon's voice was soft and mocking.

"I don't know anybody by that description."

"We heard he took up boot-making, Sheriff."

There was a pause. "So?"

"His new name is John Sevier. Maybe his reputation for making boots spread farther than was good for him."

"Yeah?" the sheriff said, and Delaplane knew by the sound of his voice that he was beaten.

Delaplane watched a woman going up the street with two boys who looked like twins. Premonition touched him. One boy ran to the edge of the walk to go around an awning post. The other bumped against the woman in his hurry to do as his brother had done.

Cold-eyed, no believer in hunches, Delaplane knew that he had been right about the woman and the two boys.

He heard the sheriff saying: "He killed the wrong man in

a political mess, but it was a fair fight. They forgot about it in Kansas."

"They didn't change the warrant. It stands."

"Two hundred and fifty dollars, Moxon! There's real bastards you can go after, worth ten times that much."

"I do my job. It's a matter of law, Sheriff."

"Law, hell! He's been here nine years, got two kids. There's not a person in town won't go the limit for him."

"It's your job to see they don't, Sheriff."

Delaplane watched the woman and the two boys come out of the boot shop. He caught a glimpse of Sevier, shaking his head slowly, pointing his wife away. The door closed, and the woman hurried down the street with the boys. Delaplane judged she was not a pretty woman.

Moxon and the sheriff came out. The sheriff was a young man, fleshy, with blue, worried eyes. He would not have lasted a full evening as a marshal in places where Delaplane had carried a badge.

The deficiency was more apparent because the sheriff was close to Moxon. The set of Moxon's lips was making puckers between the scar lumps of a powder burn near the corner of his mouth. His eyes were bright and cruel.

"I'll try," the sheriff said, "but I know he won't give up to you." He walked slowly into the bootery.

Delaplane said: "Suppose Sevier does decide to give up?" The wanted men on Delaplane's first job with Moxon had sent word to come and get them if he could.

"Sevier will stand up," Moxon said.

"Maybe he'll decide to go back and stand trial. He'd be cleared if he did."

Moxon shook his head. "There's no money in it if you have to ride five hundred miles with a prisoner."

Delaplane took a long look at Moxon and wondered

whether he was completely dead inside. He did not think Moxon was that way. In their lonely camps on the way to South Fork, Moxon had talked for hours at a time, half puzzled, half angry because men hated him. He could not understand, and it seemed that he was trying to break through his lack of comprehension so that he could walk carelessly on a street like this and be hailed in friendship, instead of being stared at in fear and hatred. Those two feelings were in the air now as men watched Moxon and Delaplane. *Bounty hunters, killers, bastards with no souls.*

The sheriff came out of the bootery. Delaplane knew by the way he hesitated that Sevier refused to give up.

"Let's get it over with," Delaplane said.

"Not so fast, son," Moxon said. "Be slow and easy. Word gets ahead, and the next job is half done for you when you get there."

Moxon liked every moment of it, the hostile attention of the town, the beaten manner of the sheriff, the fact that Sevier was inside his shop, maybe breaking up.

The sheriff came up. He gave Moxon a long stare. "He won't go back."

"Too bad," Moxon said gently.

"To you he's worth two hundred and fifty dollars. That's all you want, Moxon, so. . . ."

"Easy, youngster, I warned you once. You're about to suggest a bribe. No honest lawman. . . ."

"I'm sick of you talking about law, Moxon."

"Have a bartender mix you something, Sheriff. It'll settle your stomach." Moxon stared at the sheriff, who crossed the walk heavily and went into his office. Without turning, Moxon said: "I want affidavits of his identification, Sheriff. Get it done for me in advance or I'll have to trouble his wife about it afterward."

The man did not answer. The men of the town had deserted this side of the street. Moxon looked over at them. "They yell their heads off for law and order, but they're always thinking it's for someone else. The world is full of pious fools, Delaplane."

Silent men were dangerous. Those across the street were noisy. They reminded Delaplane of excited children. Watching them, he said: "Sevier isn't worth much, Moxon. Couldn't we . . . ?"

"No, you can't do it, not even once. Go over and get something to eat and come back."

A certain flatness followed Delaplane into the saloon, but, once he was through the doors, he heard the chattering outside resume. He ordered a beer.

"How are you, Dave?"

Delaplane swung around. The smiling man with his hand out was Frank Caldwell. He was heavier than he had been in Granada. The whiskey flush on his face was almost gone. Delaplane said: "Hello, Frank." He ignored the outstretched hand.

"What are you doing out this way?"

"Just riding." Delaplane glanced at Caldwell. There was weakness in the man's mouth. Caldwell was living proof that all Texas trail hands were not hell dogs with a double set of teeth. For a while, everyone in Granada had assumed that Caldwell was a wonder. He was appointed deputy marshal, and he had lasted three days until someone took his pistol away and threw him out of a saloon. After that, Caldwell became an odd-job man.

"It's good to see you," Caldwell said.

The bartender thumped Delaplane's beer on the bar. Some of it slopped over. Delaplane slid a silver dollar into the wetness. The bartender knocked it back.

Caldwell said: "What's the matter, Sam? Dave is a friend of mine." He said it as if it meant something, and the assumption irritated Delaplane.

"He came here with Frank Moxon."

Caldwell stared at Delaplane. "Are you with Moxon?"

Delaplane felt like slapping Caldwell as he would an insect. But Caldwell picked up the glass of beer, and they sat down at a table.

"What's on your mind, Caldwell?"

"You're not really with Moxon, are you?"

"Why not?"

"He's a bounty hunter."

"It's a job. You afraid someone will take my pistol away from me?"

The jibe didn't seem to bother Caldwell. "I wasn't cut out to be a lawman. Same as you're not a killer. Moxon is scum. He kills for money, and he enjoys it."

"You reform him."

Again, the remark didn't bother Caldwell. He was still soft and weak, but there had been a change in him. "You didn't come here after Sevier."

"Why not?"

"He's going back to Kansas to be cleared."

"He should have gone back before now."

"Dave, he killed a politician's brother. It was a fair fight, but any court would have hung him."

"I know about Sevier. He can give up."

"Moxon never delivered a live prisoner to any sheriff."

"No man is as black as he's painted."

Delaplane rose. He took the beer with him and set it before the bartender. The man's hatred was steady. Deliberately he dropped the glass into a barrel. Delaplane turned back to Caldwell who had a new kind of look on his face. Contempt? Not exactly. That would have been something, Caldwell's showing contempt of anything. But the look was disturbing. Delaplane went across to Moxon.

"The sheriff talked to Sevier again," Moxon said. "Walk past the place and take a look inside."

Time was running toward sunset. A big south window gave light on the cobbler's bench. Sevier was working. He did not look at the window when Delaplane passed. Delaplane saw big hands, a long face, brown hair. There was a pistol belt lying on the bench before Sevier.

Two hundred and fifty dollars. . . . At manhood, Sevier's boys would be worth two hundred and fifty dollars apiece. It was a crazy thought that made Delaplane uneasy. He went back to Moxon.

"He's in there alone, working on a boot."

"Pretending to, you mean?"

"No," Delaplane said. "He's really working."

A strange expression came to Moxon's face. "He ought to be shaking like a leaf."

"Look, Moxon, just this one time."

"No!" Moxon hauled out a rifle. "The sheriff's personal long gun." He gave it to Delaplane. "Some idiot will bring a horse to the back of his shop. They always try it. Cripple the horse. I'm going to eat."

Moxon went to the saloon, ignoring the men who fell back to give him room. Delaplane moved up to a hardware store. There was vacant ground on the upstreet side of the bootery and wide fire gaps between the buildings downstreet from the bootery. Delaplane waited.

He saw it coming. With over-done casualness the townsmen broke into little groups, obstructing his view through the fire gaps. But they left open spaces between their heads, and he saw the woman leading a blue roan up the alley. Sevier's wife.

Delaplane went quickly into the hardware store. He grabbed the first chair he saw and stood on it with his rifle quartered across his body. Now he could see above the heads of every man blocking the gaps. The move was prompted more because he had been challenged than because he thought Sevier actually was going to make a run for it. Sevier was not going to run.

After a time, the woman came into the shop. Her body was straight, but she broke suddenly and slumped. A gray-haired man put his arm around her and helped her down the street. Another man went into the alley and led the horse away. The groups broke up, beaten.

Delaplane sat down in the chair. He did not understand the weakness in his legs. Sevier could have made his break. He would have been hard to hit. In fact, Delaplane knew he would have missed.

The townsmen were silent momentarily when Moxon came from the saloon. Long-striding, tall, Moxon came up to where Delaplane sat.

"A chair, huh?" Moxon said. "You're catching on. Easiness always puts the fear of God into them."

He looked toward the bootery. "He's about ready to come out like a brave man. All you have to do, Delaplane, is to watch for another brave fool in that mess of magpies."

"I want to let Sevier go."

The flat gray eyes lay intently on Delaplane. "No you don't," Moxon said.

The sheriff called: "Moxon!" He was hurrying up the street with four men.

"I've seen this happen before, too," Moxon said.

The sheriff did the talking. "We've more than doubled

the reward, Moxon. Take it and leave town."

The money was in a salt sack. Moxon reached out and took it. "Five hundred, huh?"

The faces of the townsmen brightened. Standing now, Delaplane felt relief and, at the same time, disgust for Moxon. It had been only a stall to run the price up when Moxon had refused to let the sheriff mention a bribe.

Moxon hefted the sack. His smile bunched the scars on his cheek. He spread his fingers and let the money drop to the walk. "I earn my money."

It was the truth, Delaplane knew. Things people offered would never keep Moxon from the joy of killing. Delaplane had no understanding left to give Moxon.

Sevier came from the bootery, tall and deliberate. He stood, buckling around him a pistol belt.

The sheriff said: "John! Wait!" He started to run toward Sevier. He made two steps before Moxon clipped him in the side of the head with his pistol.

Habit made Delaplane swing toward the townsmen with his rifle half raised. They fell back.

"All right, Delaplane." Moxon walked toward Sevier.

"Don't, Moxon," Delaplane said. "Not this time."

"Keep your eye on them," said Moxon.

Delaplane dropped the rifle. It clattered on the street.

Moxon said: "Keep your eye on them, son. Pick up your rifle." He did not turn. His voice was under control.

Delaplane was expecting Moxon to make a simple quarter turn as he drew his pistol, but Moxon pivoted the other way, a half turn that brought him around ready to shoot. He was dead on the place where he had last heard sound from Delaplane.

The tick of time it took Moxon to shift his aim to where Delaplane now stood was the same instant Delaplane used to shoot Moxon through the heart. Delaplane saw Moxon's pistol fall. The smile lived on a split second.

Sevier's boys ran to see what was going on across the street where all the crowd was gathering.

Caldwell came through the press and took Delaplane away. Delaplane walked for a time, still gripping his pistol, before he thought to put it back into the holster.

"What changed your mind?"

Delaplane really tried to give the man an answer. He thought of a lot of things—bartenders, two boys, money in a salt sack falling on red stone—but the reddest picture in his mind was that of Moxon sitting around a campfire at night, filling the desert air with sour words and struggling to make the loneliness go away.

There was no way to put this, so he said: "I don't know." He walked with Caldwell toward the saloon.

Learn the Hard Way

They were going to hang Danny Ensign down there near the train. He would swing from the raw-yellow bridge timber the cowmen had laid from the top of the engine cab to the roof of the Sand Creek depot.

Bert Ullman was not doing anything about it; he was just lying here like a faded blue lizard, staring down through the dusty leaves of the scrub oak. Just lying there—and he had ridden with Danny for years.

It was too much for Billy Hafen—and he had been with Danny only four months. He cursed as he grabbed Ullman's arm. "They're going to lynch him, Bert!"

Ullman turned his head slowly. The flow of time had scalded gullies in his gaunt face. His thoughts came to this baking, brush-clotted hill from a long way off, and then his eyes were black chips again, and his lips took their twisted set against his teeth.

He said: "Sure, kid. The sheriff got him, but you never figured the sheriff intended to put him on that train?"

Billy Hafen stared at the scene a hundred and fifty yards away, at the spectators who had drained out of the fifteen or twenty buildings of the town, at the cowmen who were the hard core in command down there.

The engine stack coughed heat above the raw timber. Saddle horses grazed along the green-edged brightness of Sand Creek, a glittering knife slicing off toward the rabbit brush mesas below purple mountains. The sky was calm, insulting blue. There was freedom everywhere, except where tall Danny Ensign stood, hatless, roped, on the depot platform.

Two cowboys dumped the water barrel at the corner of the red building and rolled it toward the open space under the beam.

"Bert! We got to. . . ."

"Never seen a hanging, huh?" Ullman looked at Billy with savage contempt. "That barrel won't be enough, kid. Danny's got a strong neck. He'll choke there, pulling his feet up to his chest, slobbering." Ullman nodded.

"Stay down, kid!"

"If *you* won't do anything. . . ."

"Get down." Ullman's rifle barrel wagged.

Billy Hafen's cursing broke on a sob.

The two cowboys set the barrel under the beam, upside down. Morgan Campion got up on it, yelling, waving his Scotch tam. He was the one, the old hellion. He had bullied and led the other cowmen until they had brought Danny to this day.

Billy tried to grab Ullman's rifle.

"You'll get it across the side of the neck if you don't behave, kid." Ullman's eyes were dead points until Hafen rolled away.

"Why kill old Morg?" Ullman asked. "A man's got reason to be sore when his cows are stole."

I should have got him that night! Billy Hafen thought. With the same rifle Ullman was now holding. The door of the Stirrup ranch house had opened to the call, and Campion had been squat and bulky in the light. In the willows at the edge of the yard the twist of cotton on the front sight had moved up to cover his chest.

And then Billy Hafen had lost his guts. After a while Campion had gone back inside. Danny had been shouting angry when Billy told him afterward—and now Danny was going to hang because of Billy's failure.

"Follow it all the way and this is where it generally ends," Ullman said.

"Your same old talk! Shut up!" It seemed to Billy that Ullman was watching something he had hoped to see for a long time, watching, and afraid.

Campion was talking loudly. Train passengers leaned from the windows. Two women got out of the second coach, holding their skirts as they trotted around the caboose to get closer to the crowd. The conductor came over to the barrel and tried to say something, pointing up at the beam. Campion waved him off angrily.

"He'll jaw for a spell," Ullman said. "Maybe long enough for you to figure out what Danny done for you."

That didn't need figuring. Ullman was stalling because he had no guts to do anything. The sun was a hot iron on Billy's ragged jumper, pressing down like the weight of the situation below.

"He took you out of that livery stable, the only place you could get a job after the trouble your old man was in. Why'd he do that, kid?"

Sweat jerked down through the dust on Billy's cheeks as he stared at Campion, who had led the fight against Billy's father, one of the first ranchers in the San Isabel. Frank Hafen had said there was room for both ranchers and farmers.

"I should have killed him that night," Billy said. He glanced at Ullman's rifle. Bert was watching him.

"Why'd Danny pick you to join the bunch, kid?"

Ullman had always hinted it was because Danny wanted someone to get rid of Campion the easy way. That wasn't so. Danny had been sorry for a youngster no one would have anything to do with. Danny was a square-shooter.

Old Bert knew that, but he had always been jealous of Danny, always trying to hold him down. And now the fear of going against those men below was clear up in Ullman's neck, and he would not do anything but talk.

"Look at that!" Billy said.

The sheriff was walking across the bridge toward town. He beat dust from his sleeves, and then he slapped his hands together to knock dust from them. He went all the way to his office without glancing back, and the dust of his going still hung in the deserted street after he disappeared inside.

Ullman merely glanced at the incident. "I don't know whether it's worth the effort to talk to you, Billy. I've talked to a lot of them that Danny. . . ."

"You sure did! Your mouth was always going behind Danny's back. I don't know how he stood for the things you tried to pull! Always telling the younger ones they ought to get out of the bunch, to get on the other side of the fence before they were in so deep they couldn't change."

Ullman started to say something, and then he looked down the hill again. His breath went out in a long sigh. *Scared to death*, Billy thought.

Campion's voice came up. "We're the law, boys, but we're going to act right. We got to consider the evidence against Ensign before we hoist him."

Laughter rolling up the hill smashed against Billy Hafen in an obscene, sickening wave.

The coils of manila rope around Danny's middle made bright streaks against his black coat as he turned his head slowly, watching the oak thickets on the hill.

"What did you get out of your months with Danny?" Ullman asked.

Not money. That was the only way Ullman would know how to figure it. Once, after the big haul of Campion stuff on Sad Squaw, Danny had given Billy Hafen a six-gun, and promised him other things later on. It was not always so easy to collect from those mining camp butcher shops all at once, Danny had said.

Danny Ensign, a bold-nosed man with a white-streaking smile, had given Billy Hafen freedom from insults about his father; a chance to do something besides use a pitchfork in a stable; a chance to strike back at the men who had pushed his father into the grave. To hell with even trying to talk to Bert Ullman about it.

"We'll testify one at a time, boys," Campion said. "Speak up loud and don't lie about nothing."

Billy and Ullman heard the horse somewhere back in the deep part of the gulch where they lay. The sounds said it was tired. Hafen pictured the roaching back, the lather, the belly-pinching of exhaustion.

Ullman said—"Stay here."—by looking at Billy and pointing at the ground. Crouched low, Ullman took his rifle and went up the gulch like a prowling lobo.

With one eye on the red depot, Billy heard the murmur of voices a few moments later. A stirrup *clanked* when a saddle was thrown on the ground, and there came the gusty breathing of a horse too nearly dead to shake itself.

Below, Fred Clayborne, the Window Sash owner, walked over to the barrel and began to talk, pointing at Danny.

Ullman came back, with Ace Strohmeyer crouching behind him. For just a moment Billy Hafen forgot Danny.

"Ace! We heard you was dead!"

Strohmeyer pivoted with one hand reaching for the bank. He sat down heavily and leaned his head back against the forks of a branch.

He said: "Everybody that got clear of the Fossil Basin mess is here now."

But Danny was down below, and he did not look so tall now against the red boards.

"We heard they killed you at the Dutchman's . . . after you and Danny got clear of the basin," Billy said.

"Great country for rumor." Strohmeyer closed his eyes. The backs of his long hands glistened with a dry sheen on the rifle across his legs. "How much time?"

"A few minutes." Ullman shook sweat off his forehead. "Campion likes a big show." Ullman turned his head. "Still want to sight down on Campion, kid?"

"Yeah. Give me your rifle."

"You had it that night at the Stirrup. I rode into the yard and hailed him out. You didn't shoot. Why not?"

"You know I lost my sand!"

"I hoped it was because of something else." Ullman shook his head. "No, Billy, shooting old Morg now won't help Danny none. Danny won't hang, don't worry."

Suddenly there was a solid island in the floor of despair around Billy Hafen. Sure! Ullman was all right. He had pulled Danny out of scrapes before.

Back in the gulch Strohmeyer's horse went down with a *thump*. Its hoofs made scrabbling sounds in the rocks for a while, and then the gulch was still again. Engine smoke went up toward a sky that was bright with the blue of hope for Billy Hafen.

"How do we go about it, Bert?" he asked.

"I'll show you . . . when it's time."

Someone passed a parasol from a coach window to one of the waiting women. The engineer leaned from his cab. White vapor plumed from the whistle, and then the sound made Billy Hafen jump. Campion shouted angrily at the engineer.

Danny Ensign was leaning against the depot now, sort of slumped.

"What are they doing?" Strohmeyer asked. He had not opened his eyes since sitting down.

"Getting close," Ullman said. "That whistle set 'em on edge."

The whistle came again. Campion's face was red as he waved his arm at the engineer. There was a shifting and a stirring in the crowd. The woman with the parasol began to edge forward.

"We got to do it fast!" Billy said.

"Just the three of us left, huh? I'll bet we make a pretty sight." Strohmeyer cleared his throat carefully. "They put the rope up yet?"

"Not yet!" The bones were pushing hard at Ullman's tight, leathery face. "Danny couldn't get none of the rest of us to take Campion from the dark, kid. He knew you hated old Morg, besides wanting to show you was really one of the bunch."

Billy Hafen only half heard. Campion was getting off the barrel. Two men were bringing Danny forward, holding him under the arms. He was wounded! They were going to hang a wounded man!

"From the time he was fourteen," Ullman muttered. His face was the color of the rabbit brush mesas. "She knew it. I promised her to keep him out of hanging trouble."

"He's been shot," Billy said.

"No, he ain't," Strohmeyer said. "What they doing now?"

"Starting." Ullman stood up. "Cover me from here, Billy." He looked like a dead man as he went out of the scrub oak and started along the open slope.

"Wait a second!" Billy cried. "Let me. . . ."

"You stay here, kid." Strohmeyer's eyes were wide open now, the yellowish, starey eyes that had made some of the bunch say he was a little crazy, one to walk wide around. His rifle was tilted across his legs at Billy Hafen. "Bert will handle it."

"He can't . . . alone!"

"Stay here."

They had to lift Danny Ensign up on the barrel. The rope flashed over the timber above him. He yelled then and began to struggle. Riders held him where he was, with his feet drumming against the barrel.

A gush of sickness was thin and vile in Billy Hafen's mouth, but he could not look away. Old Bert was standing on the slope now, not moving, his rifle in both hands across his thighs.

"They putting it around his neck yet?" Strohmeyer asked.

"Bert ain't doing nothing!"

"He will."

"He don't care!" Billy retched. "You don't, either!"

"Bert does. Danny's his boy."

It did not sink in for a while. Billy Hafen wiped his lips and stared at Strohmeyer. One thing Ace never did was lie.

"Some men do what they can for their own blood," Strohmeyer said. "Bert tried mighty hard. He give up his ranch after Danny took to rustling, and he went along with the bunch and still kept trying." Strohmeyer's teeth made a wolf sneer in his dirty beard.

"Danny was no good, born that way. Bert was admitting that when he shifted over to working on wet-eared brats like you . . . and them two he got to quit the bunch."

Strohmeyer grunted as he held down a cough. "I never figured telling a man anything was worth the trouble. Stay down, kid. I promised Bert I'd do this much."

The yellow eyes were crazy all right. Billy looked down the hill again.

"They putting the noose on him?"

"Yes!" Campion was doing it, from a white horse that shone like wet satin. "Why'd you come here?"

Strohmeyer said: "To see him swing."

Campion snugged the knot against the side of Danny's neck. Billy groaned. "I should have killed Campion."

"You couldn't, kid. Bert pulled the powder in the shells that night. If you'd popped a primer, you'd be out there going to hell with Bert right this minute." A sodden cough came up in Strohmeyer, and it was several moments before he spoke again. "They got men on the rope now?"

Strohmeyer was enjoying this. There was no loyalty, no decency, in all the world.

The crowd was silent now. It seemed to Hafen that no one wanted to touch the free end of the rope. Then a cowboy turned it twice around his saddle horn and backed his horse away until Danny was forced to stand by himself.

The inner rim of men pressed back, clearing the space around the barrel. Danny was alone, with the hot sun striking from the clean rope that bound his arms. A mottled green and yellow parasol, clear to the front now, made a vivid mark against the drab clothes of the cowmen.

No one saw Bert Ullman standing on the slope, and Billy Hafen refused to look at him any longer.

Strohmeyer saw Billy's head go down and watched his

fingers dig like talons at the hot earth. "They're all set, huh? He's standing in the clear, is he?"

Billy had to look. Danny was on his tiptoes now. A hard line ran up from him to the yellow timber, and then slanted away to the saddle of a nervous horse.

"Kick the damned barrel out!" Campion yelled.

Three men edged forward, reaching hesitantly, and then they looked around for more support.

"Kick it over! Kick it over!" Campion roared.

Danny's cry sliced into Billy Hafen where a man holds thoughts he cannot talk about. It sent ice worms twisting through the sweat on his back. It carried despair, the squeal of cowardice, and the terror of a frightened child.

"Dad!" Danny screamed. "Dad!"

Even then no one down there but Danny knew that Ullman was standing on the hill.

"Dad!" Strohmeyer said. He laughed.

Bert Ullman raised his rifle swiftly. Its roar broke on the rocks and its sounds raced off toward the mountains. Danny's weight went dead against the rope. His knees unhinged and his body twisted sidewise until it made a true plumb line of the rope to the timber.

Except for the nervous horse, there was a frozen picture at the depot for just an instant, and then there was wildness as men knocked each other down in the confusion. The parasol disappeared. Its owner's angry scream was clear, above the shouts and yells.

The first rifle shots up the hill came from startled anger, and then they were aimed with care. Ullman staggered back against a sloping rock, bracing his legs against it, still holding his lowered rifle.

Bullets ground spray from the rock. Some of them were taking chips from stone directly behind Ullman's back. He stood until he fell, and that was only seconds.

Stupid with shock, Billy Hafen lay where he was.

"Get out of here, kid," Strohmeyer said.

The cowboy below had thrown off the turns around his saddle horn and was fighting to get his horse under control. Danny Ensign was lying on the ground, with men stumbling over him.

"Get out of here!" Strohmeyer said.

There was blood at the corners of his lips. He had not tried to move since sitting down.

Campion bellowed orders for men to flank the hill. Animal panic sent Billy Hafen up the gulch on his hands and knees. He went past Strohmeyer, and then he came back and grabbed his arm.

"Come on! I'll help you."

The evil on Strohmeyer's face was tempered with a strange expression, as if he thought it odd that any man would try to help another.

"Uhn-huh, Billy. I was dead back there at the Dutchman's. Danny. His horse was limping when they started to catch up with us."

Billy Hafen tried to pull him to his feet.

"Stop it, damn it! That hurts."

"Where you hit?"

"If you'd knowed Danny at all, you wouldn't ask. In the back, kid. Get out of here. You been chewing on meat too strong for you."

Billy Hafen started away.

"If that sorrel ain't dead, shoot the poor devil." Strohmeyer closed his eyes and let the rifle slide from his legs, muzzle first into the dust. "You got two good horses. Ride a long ways, kid, and remember what you seen today."

Billy Hafen ran up the gulch.

Join the Western Book Club
and GET 4 FREE* BOOKS NOW!
A $19.96 VALUE!

Yes! I want to subscribe
to the Western Book Club.

Please send me my **4 FREE* BOOKS**. I have enclosed $2.00 for shipping/handling. Each month I'll receive the four newest Leisure Western selections to preview for 10 days. If I decide to keep them, I will pay the Special Members Only discounted price of just $3.36 each, a total of $13.44, plus $2.00 shipping/handling ($19.50 US in Canada). This is a **SAVINGS OF AT LEAST $6.00** off the bookstore price. There is no minimum number of books I must buy, and I may cancel the program at any time. In any case, the **4 FREE* BOOKS** are mine to keep.

*In Canada, add $5.00 shipping/handling per order
for the first shipment. For all future shipments to
Canada, the cost of membership is $16.25 US,
which includes shipping and handling.
(All payments must be made in US dollars.)

NAME: _____

ADDRESS: _____

CITY: _____ **STATE:** _____

COUNTRY: _____ **ZIP:** _____

TELEPHONE: _____

E-MAIL: _____

SIGNATURE: _____

If under 18, Parent or Guardian must sign. Terms, prices, and conditions subject to change. Subscription subject
to acceptance. Dorchester Publishing reserves the right to reject any order or cancel any subscription.

The Best in Western writing!
Get Four Books FREE*–
A $19.96 VALUE!

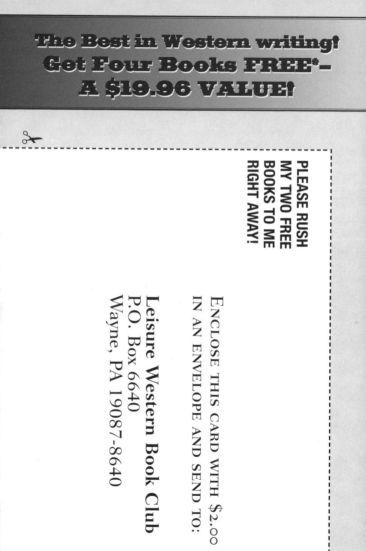

**PLEASE RUSH
MY TWO FREE
BOOKS TO ME
RIGHT AWAY!**

ENCLOSE THIS CARD WITH $2.00
IN AN ENVELOPE AND SEND TO:

Leisure Western Book Club
P.O. Box 6640
Wayne, PA 19087-8640

When Earth Gods Kill

I

In tunnel contract work, each second drips with money. On the Kokomo diversion job, Dave Cannon and Holy Gibson saved their brass sixty thousand dollars' worth of time by ignoring his orders. When he found out, he fired them both. They had worked for him for twelve years. He fired them with a minimum of words, and his only emotion was disgust.

"You cost a man's life," Brutus Shipkey said. He wrote the checks himself. "I'd rather have lost the tunnel."

Gibson, a chunky man with short, wire bristles for hair and the stubby features of a prize fighter, was one of the few real underground engineers in the United States. Big red-headed Cannon was a tunnel man, up from experience; there are no books to guide the way. The breed is rare.

Now they were nothing. The name of Brutus Shipkey lay so heavily in the world of tunnel work that no top outfit could afford to hire them, unless they wanted to be tunnel stiffs and go back to a drill or scaling bar.

Holy Gibson thought it all over for two hours. He spent

the next three days convincing Cannon that they were not done with Shipkey at all. Gibson's proposal matched his methods of engineering—use facts and proved principles as far as they will go, and then strike boldly out with common sense and guesses—and pray a little to the gods of the underground world.

"We've worked for Shipkey long enough," the engineer said. "Now let him set us up in business. With his backing, about three hundred thousand dollars' worth, we can take on the Panlap job."

"You have a large hole in your head," Cannon said. For three days he had listened to Gibson, sometimes looking at him with wonder. At last they both went to see Shipkey.

The old man sat behind an enormous desk with nothing on it but one of his elbows. What he knew of men and rock he carried in his head, and someone else could do the paperwork. A bullet head of short-cropped white hair, two tough old eyes in an old tough face. Sometimes Shipkey looked at men for five minutes without speaking, and then they often had to lean forward to catch his voice.

Linda Shipkey, his daughter, was sitting near the window. Cannon glanced quickly at Gibson; the engineer must have seen to it that she would be here. If Shipkey had a weak spot, it was his daughter. Three days ago, Cannon had a thought he was pretty close to marrying Linda. She would be expensive; she had never indicated otherwise to Cannon. She was not beautiful. Beautiful women, like engineers, were a dime a dozen in Cannon's book. But there was only one woman like Linda and only one man like Holy Gibson. Under a cap of gleaming brown hair Linda's face tended toward roundness. She had been a chubby kid when Cannon first knew her. Now she was merely full-rigged.

She was not for a tunnel stiff. The story of the inevitable

course of true love had been dropped from Cannon's reading list when he was sixteen. He was at the bottom of the hill again, and Linda was Brutus Shipkey's daughter.

So Cannon said hello as casually as Linda greeted him.

They did not have to say hello to Shipkey; he would not have answered anyway. He sat there at his desk with one side of his square face supported by the heel of his hand. He looked at them from cloudy eyes, disillusioned but not bitter. His main expression was waiting.

He put the weight of silence on them. For three days Gibson had filled the air with talk, but now he had nothing to say. On the job, Gibson went at a half trot all day long, but now he settled back into his chair, stretched out his legs, and gave the silence back to Shipkey. The engineer's attitude said: *We didn't come here to beg.*

A faint smile moved across Linda's lips. She was enjoying this.

Cannon had tried to build arguments to meet the situation. The moment was here. The arguments were no good now. He followed Gibson's lead and remained silent. It surprised him when Shipkey at last showed irritation.

"Well?" Shipkey said.

"We want the Panlap tunnel," Gibson said.

Shipkey considered that. The extensions of the engineer's flat statement began to narrow the old man's eyes, as if he could not believe what he was thinking.

"We want you to back us on the Panlap tunnel," Gibson said. "Cannon and Gibson."

"I'm damned!" the old man said intensely, so softly they barely heard him. He glanced at his daughter.

"Between the two of us we've spent a quarter of a century making you fat," Gibson said. "Now let's change sides for a while."

117

This was where they would be thrown out, Cannon thought. Twice in twelve years he had seen Brutus Shipkey blow sky-high. For several moments it appeared that the third explosion was coming.

Then Shipkey said: "So you two helped make me fat?"

He let them both remember. Cannon had been running a backhoe for a construction outfit that was going broke, and Gibson had been setting stakes, keeping time, and running errands for the same company when Shipkey took them from the jobs and began to make tunnel men of them.

Twelve years ago. He started them as scalers, men with long bars prying loose rock from the ceiling after each blast in the tunnel. They went to the drills as chuck tenders, then drillers, then walking bosses. Two years ago they had become Shipkey's right-hand men.

Shipkey sat there and let them remember.

Gibson's approach was wrong, Cannon thought. Nobody had ever bulldozed straight over Shipkey. They should try again to explain that it was not their fault a man had been killed in the Kokomo. They should start from there.

Murderers, he had called them, speaking the word calmly. They had struck bad ground in the Kokomo, soft granite filled with talc seams. Shoot short rounds and put timber in at once, Shipkey had said. They did that—it was slow, and so they drilled and shot full rounds, pulling ten feet of rock from the heading at every blast. Some soft ground will hold until the air begins to loosen it. They knew that, and they had the timber ready, rushing it forward. In one fifth of the time Shipkey had expected, they had made a thousand feet.

They were almost through the bad ground, laughing to themselves about the expression that would be on Shipkey's face when he heard the news of the money they had saved him. A scaler grew careless. Standing on the muck pile one graveyard shift, he tapped a coffin lid with his long bar. Coffin lids are great slabs of loose rock overhead. A man stands back from them, angling his bar to bring them down. Sometimes it takes no more than a touch. This one was such. The scaler merely tapped it, standing directly under it. It smashed him down into the waste pile and sprayed his blood across the shattered rock and drove the blunt end of the bar through his body. He was an experienced man and he should not have died that way. Experience breeds trust, yet rock overhead can never be trusted. A new man would have been clear by five feet and the length of his bar.

Instead of taking to Shipkey the news of progress made and money saved, Cannon and Gibson had to tell him that a man had been killed in the Kokomo—the first man ever killed on a Shipkey tunnel job.

So Brutus Shipkey fired the right-hand men who had become like sons to him, not for violating his orders, but because they had lost a man. They were in charge of the Kokomo. The scaler's death was theirs.

No, it would not do to go back again now and try to prove to Shipkey that the man might have been careless in any kind of ground. If they had not been hurrying so. . . .

There was silence in the room. Cannon looked at Linda. She met his glance squarely, and he could not tell what she thought. Linda knew tunnel work, so well that she would not talk about it to men.

"That's it," Gibson said. His stubby fighter's face was as tough as Shipkey's gaze. Holy Gibson, because he did not drink, smoke, or gamble, was tough because his mind was not hamstrung by pure intellect.

"You've got your guts, Gibson," Shipkey said. "You had

to talk Cannon into this, didn't you? What do *you* think, Cannon?"

"Stake us to the Panlap," Cannon said. "We'll run it through and make some money all around."

The old man's eyes flicked to his daughter, and then back to Cannon. "It ain't just money. That won't be enough, Cannon."

Cannon said: "Maybe not. You've ruined us, Shipkey. We'll never be top men for any outfit again as long as you hold the Kokomo against us."

"I do. I will, forever. Damn the pair of you." His expression, hard and brutal, added: *Murderers.*

They had been as sons to him because they loved the same work he loved. He had taught them what they knew of tunnel work, never showing them affection or mercy. *Nor would he now,* Cannon thought. They had betrayed not him, but the values he stood for: If you can't hold things without crippling or killing men, you don't belong in construction.

Twelve years wiped away. Cannon stared at the old man's face. Not everything of those twelve years could be cast aside so quickly. But there was nothing on Shipkey's face that said otherwise.

Cannon said: "We can finish the Panlap. You know how bad the country needs lead and zinc."

"Don't wave any flags at me," Shipkey said. "What you mean is you two need a job. You got the guts of a government mule to think I would use my money to back. . . ."

"Yes, we need the job," Gibson said. "We need it from you. You're the one that wrecked us, and you're the one that had better give us a chance, or else no outfit in the country will want us as anything but tunnel stiffs."

"I know that," Shipkey said. "I'm satisfied."

"We're not," Cannon said. "We're better tunnel men

than you ever were. We can prove it on the Panlap. You quit that job."

"Their money ran out!"

"You would have quit anyway," Gibson said. "I know you didn't want to take any chances with men's lives. We can put the Panlap through and never lose a man."

"The hell you can. You don't know what that tunnel is."

"It won't take us long to find out," Cannon said.

"You owe us the chance," Gibson said.

"I owe you . . . ," Shipkey choked in anger.

They had him, Cannon thought—whenever anyone jarred him away from his coldness, he could be maneuvered.

They went to work on him deliberately. They insulted him; they challenged him. *It was the only way,* Cannon thought. He saw Linda's eyes grow dark with anger and knew she would make him pay for this later.

At last Shipkey said: "All right. You can have the Panlap, on my terms. The minute there's a serious injury, you two are done. I mean you're promising now never to work a tunnel job again, in any capacity, if you get anybody smashed up on the Panlap."

"To hell with that," Cannon said.

"Tunnel men." Shipkey smiled grimly. "A two-bit engineer who guesses his way through rock, and a shovel operator who'd like to marry my daughter. I thought you'd drop your tails and run."

Something had slipped. Shipkey was on top now. In fact, he had been on top all the time, Cannon decided.

Gibson said: "We can do it your way. You won't see us hightailing it from the first run of dolomite sand."

"Is that a fact?" The square-cut old face hardened. "You'll spile that sand, won't you? That's a word you two never heard of before I took you off a Joe McGee road job. You might be able to do that." He looked at Cannon. "Do you take it or not? You were begging hard enough a minute ago."

It was an effort for Cannon not to look at Linda. "All right. We'll take it."

Shipkey said softly: "The sand is nothing. There's something else about the Panlap. Of course, it won't take long for a smart pair like you to find out everything, will it?"

They stood on the curb outside. Cannon had an uneasy feeling that they had not put anything over. They had been in South America when Shipkey Construction started the Panlap, but they had heard the rumors that the old man was glad to drop the job.

"Just sand?" Cannon asked.

"The sand, lots of water . . . I don't know what else. You know how the old man keeps his mouth shut. We'll find out."

The hard way, Cannon thought. *When any job threw Brutus Shipkey.* . . . He watched a cop writing a parking ticket for Gibson's station wagon.

"Somehow he got us over a barrel," Gibson said. "But we'll show him."

They walked on down the street to the station wagon. Gibson didn't see the ticket until he was inside. Shipkey's car was just ahead, and the flag was down on the meter. The cop glanced at it casually and went on.

II

The Panlap mining district was a gigantic basin lying ten thousand feet high. Its smelters were long dead, the gallows frames above its shafts were rotten, the twenty thousand who had been here when lead and zinc came from the earth day and night were now less than one hundred, old men puttering in neat gardens among the ruins.

Pumping water had always been a fearful problem in the Panlap mines. Few workings had lasted long below eighteen hundred feet. The ore was still down there, and so was the water.

When the need for lead and zinc was acute during the Second World War, the Panlap drainage tunnel had been started four airline miles from the basin. It was planned to come under Panlap seven hundred feet below the average depths of the mines, to drain the workings, to make available untold tons of needed metal, to serve as a central working passage to all the great producers. It was not finished before the war ended—there seemed to be no great need for it then. Demobilize everything. But wars do not end, and now there was both need and money once more.

Cannon & Gibson, a brand new name in tunnel contract work. Their contract had a time limit, not set by Brutus Shipkey, but put there by the companies who were putting up the money to reclaim the flooded Panlap district.

They started where the others had quit—in the sand. Dolomite sand is so fine it runs like water, and it seems to run forever. In the Panlap region it is a hellish problem underground. Sometimes tunnels are run around the areas filled with sand, but the detouring is a matter of chance—the sand may be worse to the right or left.

Cannon and Gibson went straight through. They spiled. Around the sides of timber sets and over the caps they drove with pneumatic hammers almost one hundred thousand board feet of three inch planks before they ran through the sand to hard granite. Progress went by inches against the ever-flowing grains. It cost them time and money.

Somewhere above them was a mighty void where sand had poured away, but they were timbered safely down here. Let the concrete men who would come later have their little problems, also.

Shipkey came to see the tunnel a dozen times, arriving at any hour, asking no one's permission to go in. He found little things wrong here and there. One stretch of airline was not pegged properly to the wall; it might fall and injure someone; there were loose fishplates in the track; the pipe of an oil stove in the bunkhouse was not insulated where it went through the wall.

They corrected those trifling errors, but each time Shipkey came, he found a few more minor oversights. Cannon and Gibson climbed their safety man—he worked hard, but Brutus Shipkey had been driving tunnels before the safety man was born, and so the old man could always find a few details to point his finger at.

Shipkey never mentioned the sand they had gone through. He did not ask how deep they were. He knew. His quietness implied that he knew much more about the Panlap than they ever would.

"He makes me nervous," Gibson said. "He's too damned quiet."

Cannon was suspicious, too, but he had time to wonder why Linda never came with her father. Maybe that was the punishment for trying to browbeat the old man to get this job.

It went too well. Day after day the white X that Gibson

painted on the tunnel breast to mark the center of the bore was transit-straight toward the planned heading under Panlap. They were in more than three and a half miles. In two places they had to drill holes into the walls of the bore and pump concrete under pressure to reduce bursts of water that lay across the tunnel in sheets. That cost time, but they were still ahead of the game. Gibson was suspicious when things went too easily, and Cannon was edgy when one problem did not follow soon upon another. They kept remembering Shipkey's quiet confidence, his lack of questions.

"What have we overlooked?" Cannon asked.

Gibson said: "I've tried to check from hell to breakfast. I don't know."

Then, in two days, the volume of water running in the ditch under the track jumped from seven thousand gallons a minute to twelve thousand. That was nothing in the Panlap district; several of the deeper mines had pumped three times as much day and night.

Gibson did not like it. "What's the name of that first mine we go under?"

"The Buffalo . . . Elk . . . the Coyote . . . hell, look at the map."

Gibson took the sheets off the rack. "The Wolf. It says here nineteen hundred feet to the bottom level." He frowned. "We'll be under that all right, but where's all the water been coming from already?"

"This country floats on water," Cannon said. "We've crossed a drainage fissure. Of course, we're getting some Wolf water."

"We're getting too much all at once."

"Yeah." Vague worry based on remembrance of Shipkey's quietness ran in Cannon. "Let's go dump some chloride of lime in the Wolf, and see how fast it comes through."

They drove to the old workings at the lower end of the Panlap Basin. The lower levels of the Wolf had been abandoned fifty years before, the upper levels kept open to desultory leasing for twenty years longer. The shaft was a crumbling glory hole in the middle of dumps that covered acres. There were rock and mortar boiler foundations still standing. Out from the shaft, dark rot stains on the gray waste marked the fallen gallows frame.

Gibson walked around the dumps. "She was a whopper. There must be workings down there to chill your blood." He hunched his shoulders as if sudden cold had come down from the peaks. "Shaft work! I wouldn't have liked that."

"Who made that map that says nineteen hundred feet, Holy?"

"That young engineer who chased around with Linda during the war. He gathered up all the dope on the Panlap mines for Shipkey."

"Was he any good?"

Gibson grinned. "Linda turned him down when you came back from South America. The old man fired him."

"How'd he know how deep the Wolf is? There wasn't a single level map of it in that bunch of papers Shipkey gave us."

They looked at each other for several moments. A whisper of wind ran across the enormous waste piles, and a cold thought lay between the two men.

"You're thinking it could be deeper . . . right in our way down there?" Gibson asked. "Don't crowd us, Dave. We haven't got too much clearance now."

"If it's deeper, we've got to know."

Gibson stared at the funneled collar of the old shaft. He

said: "We've got to know exactly."

They dumped ten sacks of chloride of lime down the sloping sides. They heard the sullen *choom!* of water far below. Surface water, underground water—the eternal snows on the mountain soaked into the earth. Every mine in the basin was a tremendous reservoir. There would be in the bottom of the Wolf caved rock, jackstraw tangles of fallen timbers, the mud and slime of fifty years. No manual method of measurement would work.

Gibson shook his head. "I remember now. I wrote the Wolf heirs for any dope they had. All they knew about the Wolf was that it made a lot of people rich . . . and then they asked how long it would take to drain after we drove the Panlap through." His eyes were tight. "Let's find an oracle."

They went past blocks of dead houses in Panlap before they found a human being. He was not old enough to have worked deep in any of the mines, and he did not have the look, either, but they stopped to talk to him.

"Do you know any of the old-time miners here?" Cannon asked.

The man had a ready grin. "Uhn-huh. I'm more interested in the ones that will come when that tunnel below camp begins to open things up here again. I'll be ready for them."

"Beer joint, cathouse . . . one thing and another, huh?" Gibson made his disgust clear.

"That's the general idea," the fellow said. "You know exactly how long they're going to be on the tunnel? I've heard. . . ."

"It's a ten-year job," Gibson said. He drove on down the street.

They found two old men who knew nothing of the Wolf.

They had worked only at the Elk, they said, which was good enough for anybody.

One of them said: "Try Joe Detwiler. He used to be at the Wolf, I think."

Joe Detwiler was picking raspberries from bushes shoulder high beside a white painted house. He was a wrinkled neck stemming up from a gray woolen jacket, a pair of watery brown eyes under the brim of a new felt hat with a feather in the band.

"The Wolf? I was boss timberman there for over twenty years." A bleakness touched his face. He sat down on his porch with the pan of raspberries in his lap. "You fellows from the tunnel?"

They introduced themselves. His grip was weak; his hand thin and narrow.

"How deep is the Wolf shaft?" Gibson questioned the old man. "Do you know?"

Detwiler shook his head. "You ever hear of old Brutus Shipkey?"

"Yeah," Cannon said.

"Well, he wanted to know that, too, not long after the tunnel was started the first time. I couldn't tell him. Big Jack Robey couldn't tell him, and Jack worked on the bottom level before it was flooded out."

"You must have heard a figure," Gibson said.

"Sure," Detwiler said. "Around twenty-two hundred feet, but I couldn't guarantee that. Jack Robey says that's about right, but he admits he don't know for sure."

Gibson's green eyes held Cannon in a narrow grip. If the Wolf was twenty-two hundred feet, it was squarely in their way, and the Panlap drainage tunnel was headed into death with every slam of the drills.

This, then, must be what had made Shipkey so sure and quiet.

"We have a map that indicates nineteen hundred feet," Gibson said. "I'm wondering. . . ."

Detwiler said: "I can tell you who made your map. A young slick-boot engineer that worked for Brutus Shipkey. He measured the Wolf shaft with a wire and a lead weight." Detwiler smiled. "What he didn't know was about the leasers who gouged around the upper levels for years after the mine was flooded out below the tenth level. You know leasers. They dumped their muck down the shaft. All they ever hoisted was ore."

"Didn't you tell the engineer that?" Cannon asked.

"He never asked. He was a smart lad and he didn't need answers from old duffers like me and Jack."

They went to see Big Jack Robey. His shack was filled with pictures from the days when he had been a double-jack drilling champion. He was eighty-one now, a great frame with the flesh sagged away, but still the semblance of an athlete's grace in his movements.

"Twenty-two hundred, I think," he said. "A hoist man could say for sure, but all the Wolf hoist men who worked there when the bottom was open are gone now."

"A drift east of the bottom?" Gibson asked.

"There was, only to the east. The richest ore in the camp came from there. We worked like fiends in water that was never lower than your knees, no matter how good the pumps were working. One night a pump played out. The water was chest-deep before we got out of the drift and up the ladder to the next level. They fought it out just one summer, as I recall, before the water got too much for us. There's a five-foot breast of ore down there yet. I mean it."

"Stope above the bottom level?" Cannon asked.

Robey shook his head. "We never had time to stope."

"How far east does that drift run, Mister Robey?" Gibson asked.

"I can't be sure, of course. A man forgets some things and then makes up answers that seem natural. But I recall it was anyway two hundred feet. It seemed longer the night the water almost got us."

They talked very little on the way back to the camp at the portal of the Panlap tunnel.

Linda was in the office. She took one look at their faces. "So you found out about the Wolf?"

"You knew, then?" Cannon asked.

"Yes."

"Your old man didn't hold out a set of maps on us, did he?" Cannon was angry.

Linda threw her anger back at him. "That's a stinking thing to say! I crawled through half the attics in this state trying to find level maps of the Wolf during the last war. I've still been trying for you two."

"I'm sorry," Cannon said. "I knew old Brutus wouldn't do a thing like that. Did he go in?"

Linda nodded.

Gibson was already putting on his rubber clothing.

They went in on the bulldog, the squat electric engine that moved all tunnel traffic. Behind them the square of portal light grew smaller and smaller. Under them the gushing water sounded endlessly. They went a little more than three miles, to the last big station back from the breast.

Silent Anderson was there, greasing his mucking machine. He nodded. They left the bulldog and went on toward the heading. And now the belting clamor of the drills came to them stronger and stronger. The lights strung on the ceiling could not kill all the dripping gloom of the underground. The dark and wetness belong down there and they let a man know always that he is the intruder.

At the sound-shocked heading on the bore, Shipkey was standing beside a battery of floodlights directed on the steel staging and the two teams of drillers. On the top deck Evan Perko changed steel in Spud Tipton's drill, guiding the new steel into the hole. The air was slamming again almost before the chuck was locked. It was deft, savage, quick—tunnel work.

Shipkey saw the two men come up. He studied their faces for a moment. He nodded, and then he looked once more at the black-garbed drillers, surrounded by their thunder and a gauzy curtain of vaporized oil blown down the airlines to lubricate the drills.

Gibson dipped his hand into the water. He smelled, and then he tasted. He looked quickly at Cannon. The chloride of lime they had dumped into the Wolf was here already. Down through the ancient crevices, down from the mighty column of the shaft.

Shipkey looked at them without expression. The floodlights threw a shifting gleam on water dripping from his hard-boiled hat. Gibson pointed straight ahead. His lips formed the word Wolf. Shipkey nodded: *Of course*. With the taste of the ice water on his lips, with the cold feel of terror creeping into him, Shipkey looked at the breast. Every biting turn of the drills was putting them closer.

Picture the Wolf waiting there ahead, a great trunk coming down more than two thousand feet from the surface, with all the levels standing from the stem like horizontal branches, and then between those levels were vertical raises and tremendous slopes where ore had been removed. Touch the Wolf anywhere and it would explode its cold water into the Panlap, driving its débris before it like shot down a barrel. It would gut the Panlap.

The thunder of the drills washed over Cannon. Gibson's mouth was tight as he stared ahead, trying to see through rock. Old Brutus watched them calmly. Until they knew otherwise, they must accept the miners' figure of twenty-two hundred feet, which meant they were not sure of anything about the Wolf.

The drills chewed rock and splashed it from the holes and drove deeper into the streaming breast.

Cannon tapped Gibson's shoulder. He made a slash mark in the air to indicate the Wolf shaft. He made accordion motions with his hands, asking: *How far to the right of the shaft are we?*

One-two-five, the engineer signaled. One hundred and twenty-five feet.

The figure, Cannon knew, was based on the assumption that the Wolf shaft was vertical, like all the major shafts in the Panlap district. They had then ample clearance of the trunk, but there was still the bottom drift, or level.

Robey remembered it as extending about two hundred feet to the east. Cannon made the accordion motions vertically. Gibson held one forefinger horizontally to indicate the drift, and then he punched his other forefinger against it. That said: *We'll run straight into the level.*

They were already too close to the Wolf to make a turn without dropping back. There was no time for that. Cannon could not accept defeat, but defeat kept staring at him. And Shipkey, who had let them stick their necks into a noose, watched their futile signals and made none of his own. What had he wanted? Why had he done it? Cannon did not know. They had angered him, yes, and they had put a blood blemish on his reputation. That was not enough.

III

All three of them went back to the bulldog. The operator took them grinding down the rails. Sunlight hit them like a blow, and still they had not spoken. Linda was talking to an electrician on the dump. She followed them into the office.

Gibson said: "We know why you were glad to drop this job, Shipkey. We learned that much, anyway."

"Uhn-huh," Shipkey said. "You're running blind and you finally found it out. What are you going to do?"

"We'll find out if the damned shaft really is twenty-two hundred feet deep," Cannon said.

"Fine! Do that." Shipkey let them consider the fact that he had not been able to find out anything about the Wolf.

Linda said: "There must be accurate maps somewhere."

"There may have been . . . once." Shipkey glanced at his daughter, and then he looked at Cannon.

Cannon had never known how the old man felt about marriage between him and Linda.

"You didn't stop the drills," Shipkey said. "You don't know where you're headed, and you didn't stop the drills. I won't stand for that. I'll shut you down."

All the stubbornness in Gibson flared. "You don't know how deep down the shaft is! We may be clear under that bottom level."

"You're not going to slam ahead and find out by killing men," Shipkey said. "I can take the tunnel over, make the turn, and finish it. There won't be any money in it, but there won't be any blood, either."

"Is that what you figured all the time?"

"You ought to know better."

"What did you figure then, damn you!"

Shipkey was not to be angered today. He smiled.

"You're the two big-shot tunnel men that did all the figuring, as I remember. You were better tunnel men than me."

"You can't take it away from us," Gibson said.

"Yes, I can. Read your contract again. If I have to step in here, you two will be not only men who couldn't cut the buck for me, but also a pair of big mouths that fell flat on the first job they tried on their own."

"You're not going to do it!" Gibson said.

"Not for a while. How far from the Wolf are you?"

"A hundred and sixty-three feet, this shift," the engineer said.

"If you haven't got sense enough to back up, I'll let you go half that distance," Shipkey said. "Then I'm stopping you from killing somebody. I've got time . . . you haven't. I can put deep holes out toward the Wolf, if I want to. In three or four months, it'll drain."

"I think, by God, you planned to do that," Gibson said.

Shipkey walked to the door. "Come on, Linda."

She hesitated until the old man was gone. "What do you think?" she asked Cannon.

"We asked for it. We got it."

"I mean about my father."

"To hell with him," Cannon said. "I'm thinking about Gibson and me."

"That sounds natural enough," she said.

Cannon looked at her for several moments. He saw old Brutus in her and he saw the woman in her, and the woman looked at him much longer. But they were old enough to know that love can fall over little obstacles, as well as mountains. The Wolf stood, also, between him and Shipkey's brat.

Linda said: "I'll see you." She went out.

Cannon sat down on his desk. "Where do we start?"

"We find out for sure how deep the Wolf is."

Shipkey and his daughter drove across the dump and up the hill.

Joe Detwiler and Big Jack Robey were the only two men in Panlap who were survivors of the Wolf; they knew of no other living man who had worked there. To the best of their knowledge, the shaft was twenty-two hundred feet deep, and the drift that lay athwart the progress of the Panlap tunnel was two hundred feet long. Cannon was sure they were talking as honestly as their memories would serve them.

In desperation the contractors went again to the Wolf. They dropped long timbers across the collar and made a small platform, from which they unreeled steel wire with a ten-pound lead weight on the end.

It went down and down into the icy depths of the shaft. One thousand on the mark, fifteen, sixteen, seventeen hundred feet. The wire went slack between seventeen and eighteen hundred. They could not work the weight on past the obstacle down there.

"Jammed timbers choking the shaft," Cannon said. "She's come apart that much more since the last measurement that engineer took."

Black water waiting. The dumps were enormous. Each cubic foot of waste up here was water down below, with no account of the ore also hoisted. Far below the drills were still beating rock, driving closer to death.

"We're done," Cannon said. "Why don't we admit it?"

"I know it," Gibson said, "but I can't admit it. I got you into this, Cannon."

"No. Shipkey got us both into it."

They began to reel in the wire.

"I was thinking of you and Linda," Gibson said.

"So was I. It's a habit I'd better break."

They did not hurry back to the portal—there was no use to try for footage records now.

"Why'd he do it?" Gibson asked. "I used to think there wasn't another man in the world like old Brutus."

"He didn't change any. We lost him a man, and then we tried to push old Brutus around. It's just never been done, that's all."

"He was like a father once," Gibson said. "A damned tough father, but one that you can appreciate after you've lost him."

They went to the heading. The drillers and chuck-tenders were hunched against the steady pour of water. Spud Tipton cut his air. He leaned out from the deck and signaled the driller below. Silence was deadly—it spoke of defeat. There was just the *hissing* of the air couplings and the steady pour of water.

"She's stinking of an old mine, Cannon," Tipton said. "I can smell rotten timbers and slime and. . . ."

"We got noses!" Gibson said. "Run your drill."

"This old Wolf mine ahead . . . there's been some talk. . . ."

Cannon said: "We'll let you know, Spud. Nobody is going to get smashed."

"You're damned right," Tipton said. "I ain't going to get caught in here. I'm quitting on this round."

"Got it up in your neck, huh?" Cannon said.

Deep in its ancient seams, the earth groaned, then sent rapping noises. Tommy-knocking, old-time miners call the sounds, the ghostly signaling for help of all men killed underground, whose bodies still lie beneath the rock. Down through the centuries the Tommy-knockers have rapped for succor, to see the light again.

The drillers knew the sounds for what they were, the endless settling of the underground, and they also knew the legend. Their eyes rolled white as they looked at the breast and smelled the odor of the Wolf and listened to the water.

"I got it up in my neck, yeah," Tipton said.

"Stay with it a few more days," Gibson said.

Going toward the station, Cannon said: "What was the use?"

"What's the use of sitting on our tails and whining? We'll go as far as we can." Gibson was sore enough to slam head-on into the Wolf.

Cannon said: "We're not trying any by-guess and by-God deals of yours, Holy."

"We're going to give up, huh?"

"What else have you got to do?" Cannon was angry, too. "If we tap the Wolf, we'll lose twenty men in seconds. We'll lose everything."

"We lose anyway."

They let it go at that, walking on in silence, suddenly hating each other with the unreasoning force that only kinship or long friendship can give to anger.

A walking boss at the bulldog station told them Linda Shipkey was outside and had phoned in for them.

Cannon saw the excitement on her face at once. She hauled him toward her car. The back seat was covered with old maps and papers. "The Wolf!" she said.

Gibson had already jerked open the door and was grabbing.

"One of the Wolf heirs I talked to said his father used to live in Aspen. I found these in the attic of an old carriage house over there. I took everything, maps, time books, records . . . even two rolls of old wallpaper."

Gibson trotted toward the office with his arms full of papers. "Bring everything!" he yelled.

They unrolled the level maps, sheet after sheet of faded blue. The Wolf was there in hard white lines and sloping letters, the mighty cavities of stopes between the levels, and drifts that ran a thousand feet on both sides of the stem that was the shaft.

"Some mine," Gibson muttered.

A terrible pile of water, Cannon thought.

The shaft went down with every sheet they turned; with every turning their eyes shot first to the figure at the bottom of the trunk. And then all the sheets were read and the three did not look at each other for a moment. There was no map for anything below nineteen hundred and seventy-two feet, but broken white lines on the last sheet ended at twenty-one hundred feet, where neat letters said: **Present Working Depth.** That was for the year of 1900.

Linda said: "Hell, I thought I'd done something useful."

"You did all right," Gibson said. His anger was gone now. "I doubt that there ever was a map of the bottom. The idea was to get the ore, and to hell with any record of where it came from. What you got here is unusual. Maybe we can. . . ."

"Don't strain yourself, Holy," Linda said. "We've all been let down with a bang."

"Take a walk, you two," Gibson said. "I'm going to get something out of this mess if I have to draw it in myself."

Linda said: "You probably will . . . and Dave will back you up."

She walked with Cannon on the sun-bright dump, past the piles of rails and ties and timbers that would never be needed by Cannon and Gibson in the Panlap.

The word about the Wolf was out. Top men and electricians, testing for a break in a long cable spread on the waste, watched Cannon uneasily. Tunnel stiffs are men who accept the hazards of a very special occupation, learning to use their fear as protection against carelessness. But the fear is always there, and now they knew about the Wolf. There was only one way to run in the Panlap, out. Three and one half miles. The fear was healthy.

"You wanted us to get through, didn't you?" Cannon said.

"Why wouldn't I want you to?"

There is success in failure, sometimes, but it was not there for Dave Cannon. The Wolf was there, instead, between him and Linda, the patient, waiting Wolf, holding hard to the cold secret of its thousands of tons of water. In a flash of blinding, bitter anger, Cannon thought of how well the mine had been named.

He said: "Old Brutus didn't want us to make the grade, did he?"

"Why not?"

"He didn't tell us about the Wolf."

"No, you two started to tell him everything there was about the Panlap, first."

"Would you have married me if we had made it here?"

"You sound like you've given up."

Cannon eyed her narrowly. "Do you know anything that says it isn't hopeless?"

"No, I don't."

"My first question was. . . ."

"You put it on the wrong basis, Dave. I wouldn't even try to answer it."

"Well, what the hell basis . . . ?"

"I'm tired, Dave. I was up all night, driving. I won't stand out here and quarrel with you, not the way you feel right now."

When Cannon returned to the office, Gibson was still scowling at the maps. "Why'd she beat it so quick?"

"She's worn out. She headed for that little tourist camp in Panlap."

Gibson did not take his eyes from the maps. "If I wanted a woman, Dave. . . ."

"I know. Old Drive Ahead Gibson. You'd marry her, in spite of everything. That's talk, Holy. That's something to make the ribbon clerks wiggle and beat their chests."

"Yeah, it is." Gibson forgot the whole matter in an instant. "So far, we haven't got a thing here."

Still thinking of Linda Shipkey, Cannon picked up a payroll record. The figures bored him instantly. He took a foreman's time book for 1885. The leaves were brittle, the ink faded brown. He read the names of forgotten men, the records of shifts worked in a dead century, slanting lines that marched in tiny boxes toward the end of months.

In June 1885, three men had not finished their shift. Killed on 14th level. Cannon put the book aside.

Shipkey's father and his grandfather had died in another mine when Shipkey was a boy, killed in the same manner by a cave-in. Old Brutus never talked of them, or of the old, brutal days of mining. Maybe his uncompromising attitude toward safety was a living memorial to men and events never mentioned in talk.

Gibson glanced up. "Don't sit there, staring! Keep digging as long as there's anything to read in this mess!" He returned savage attention to the maps.

Drainage from the Wolf was stinking up the whole

tunnel; they did not know where they were, and here they sat looking at musty papers. Cannon picked up another time book. It was a record of top men—the surface workers, timber-framers, hoist-men, dump trammers, blacksmiths, boiler men, and others. He found several more time books that listed top men, and then the continuity of the years was broken, the last record jumping to 1900. One hoist-man's name, Mike Stanfield, was in all the books. Cannon wrote down his name and the names of all the other hoist-men.

He said: "If we could find one of these men still alive he might be able to tell us exactly how much cable went down the Wolf."

Gibson nodded. "Try Detwiler and Robey again."

IV

The old miners were sitting in the sunshine on Robey's porch, framed by the ruins of the flooded mines and the sagging shacks of Panlap.

"Tim Hanna? Yeah," Detwiler said. "He run the big new hoist we got in 'Eighty-Seven, for about six months. One night in winter he went up to grease the main sheave wheel. There was ice on the ladder. He slipped. The shaft doors weren't automatic then, and they were open."

"She was about fifteen hundred feet deep then," Robey said. "You remember, Joe . . . we wouldn't let his widow and kids see him?".

"I remember."

Cannon went through the list of hoist-men who had worked at the Wolf. There were some the miners did not remember. There were others they knew were dead, because Robey and Detwiler had been at the funerals.

"This Mike Stanfield was there a long time," Cannon said. "Would he be alive today?"

"He was the best," Detwiler said. "He never jerked a cage, he never missed a signal. Mike was a dandy. His daughter took him away from here twenty years ago, I guess it was." He shook his head. "No, he wouldn't be alive."

"You're sure he isn't?"

"He was fourteen years older than me," Robey said. "He was a thin fellow, and he always had trouble with his stomach. He used to drink goat's milk from the herd old Austrian John ran over in Poverty Gulch. I remember one time when those goats got into Bill Enright's shack. . . ."

"Do you *know* that Stanfield is dead?"

"He must be," Robey said. "I remember helping him into the car when his daughter came after him. He didn't weigh ninety pounds. Her name was Jason then. I knew her from when she was a little girl. She married this Jason, and he lost his money in a muskrat farm, and then he up and died of pneumonia one winter. . . ."

"Where did she take him?" Cannon asked.

"Big Bend, I think it was," Detwiler said. "Somewhere down there in the valley. Big Bend or Riverton. I think she married again after Vince Jason died."

Cannon's car pulled into the Sunset tourist court just behind Shipkey's black sedan. The Sunset was a half dozen slab-sided cabins and a café of sorts for tourists who took the ten-mile detour from the main highway to prowl the ruins of Panlap.

Shipkey was sitting on a bench near the gas pumps, talking to the elderly man who ran the place. Relaxed, grinning about something, wearing old clothes, Brutus Shipkey could have been taken for an inhabitant of the ghost town.

For one sharp instant Cannon felt that there was too much age in the world, and that it was all weighted against youth. He went over to Shipkey.

"Did Linda tell you about the maps, Brutus?"

"Yeah." The old man appeared irritated by this intrusion on his trivial conversation with the camp owner. "What are you going to do now?"

"I'm looking for a hoist-man who worked at the Wolf when the cage went all the way."

Shipkey pursed his lips dubiously. "You're starting that a little late. You must not have more than thirty feet left to where I told you to stop."

"Where's Linda?"

"Number Two." Behind Shipkey's cloudy eyes there lay rapid calculation and a weighing.

He would be at the tunnel from now on to the end, Cannon knew, waiting to prevent Gibson from driving beyond the limit Shipkey had set. As Cannon walked away, he heard the two men resume their conversation. They were talking about famous trotting horses.

Linda was wearing brown slacks and a brown suede jacket with fringing. When she called for Cannon to come in, she was stooping to see her face in a low mirror while she put on make-up. She did not look around at him.

"I'm going down into the valley to see if I can find a hoist-man," Cannon said. "I don't know how long I'll be. Tell Gibson, will you?"

She turned slowly and looked at him. "Let Brutus do that. I'll go with you, Dave."

Standing beside Cannon's car a few minutes later, Shipkey looked at his daughter without expression. "I guess you know what you're doing," he said.

She slept all the way down the pass and into the sticky evening heat of the valley. Looking at her resting there in the angle of the seat back and door, Cannon wondered why he had not asked her to marry him long ago, before his life became involved with everything that stemmed from a scaler's careless moment in the Kokomo. Now, as she had said, the matter was resting on a wrong basis, failure or success of the Panlap.

Neon glare in the narrow streets of Riverton began to rouse Linda. She was fully awake when Cannon stopped in front of the police station.

"How old would your hoist-man be?" she asked.

"A hundred and fifty or so. About as old as you look right now."

"Go to hell," she said cheerfully.

The night chief was a huge gray-haired man. He looked at Linda more often than he looked at Cannon. There had been a Vince Jason here, maybe ten years ago, he said. It seemed to the chief that the man had died or moved away. He made a phone call and a woman's sharp voice rattled the line for several minutes after his first question.

The chief hung up. "Vince Jason died in the middle 'Thirties. His wife married a man named Cromwell. Her father was living with her then. He was an old Panlap miner, all right. They all moved to Big Bend or Red Coulée about ten years ago."

Cannon and Linda drank coffee. "We've gained ten years already," he said. "Stanfield left Panlap twenty years ago."

"We'll rent another car," Linda said. "We can check on each other through the police stations."

Alone, Cannon sent his car whining through the night to

144

Red Coulée. By nine o'clock in the morning he was satisfied that no one in Red Coulée knew of a miner named Mike Stanfield or his daughter, a Mrs. Cromwell. He fell asleep in the police station, after his call to Big Bend told him Linda had not checked in yet.

She called him at eleven o'clock. Mrs. Cromwell had died in Big Bend nine years before. No one there knew anything of an aged father.

"She has two daughters in California," Linda said, "and a niece in a little place about sixty miles from here, Standard. I'll try there, after I get a few hours sleep."

Cannon said he would drive over to Big Bend to meet her. In the back of his mind he held the quest for Mike Stanfield a lost cause, but he would run it out to the end. He thought of Gibson, trying desperately to wrest something from the maps.

In a few hours the drills in the Panlap would be dead. There would be nothing but the sound of water. Old Brutus would take the job, negotiate a new contract, and let time be his ally. Cannon and Gibson could slink away.

Time and their own over-eagerness had smashed them, Cannon thought. He stood in front of the police station. His eyes were heavy and red, his stomach burning from too many cigarettes. The thought of sleep was repugnant.

Time.

Silent drills in the Panlap. Old Brutus looking at Cannon and Gibson without malice, without triumph, merely letting them know what they were—failures that could have been otherwise. Shipkey taught his lessons the hard way.

On the way to Big Bend the whine of the engine was hypnotic. Six or seven times Cannon had to get out and walk along the highway to keep from dozing at the wheel.

Linda was gone when he got to the Big Bend police station. He called the hotels and found the one where she had stayed three hours and then checked out. A desk sergeant regarded the unshaven man suspiciously.

"She said she'd call you here. You may as well wait."

An hour later the call came for Cannon.

"Dave!" Linda said. "I've found him! Meet me here at the Standard Hotel."

They went to the white three-storied building on a dusty street at the edge of Standard. It was called a convalescent home; it was a place where the old and the unwanted go to die. Mike Stanfield lay on a hospital bed, a bone-gray face against the pillow. His eyes were closed.

The matron, an angular woman in a blue uniform, said: "Mike! Mike! There's visitors for you."

One of Stanfield's eyes was blank. The desolation of the Wolf lay behind the film of the other, which for a while did not see Cannon or Linda or anything else.

"He's ninety-six," the matron said, either proudly or with awe.

Intelligence began to turn away the film on the old man's one good eye as he stared at Cannon. "I don't place you, boy, but I'm getting to where I sometimes can't remember like I used to." He said a name that was not Cannon's.

Unless they lay in the long ago, names would mean nothing to Mike Stanfield, Cannon thought. "We're going under Panlap with a drainage tunnel, Mister Stanfield. The Wolf mine is in our way. I talked to Jack Robey and Joe Detwiler about it. . . ."

"Big Jack. Now there's a man for you. When he goes up on the rock to drill, bet your money, boy." Stanfield smiled and fell asleep.

The woman in blue wakened him again.

"When the cage is at the bottom level of the Wolf, how much cable is down the hole?" Cannon asked.

The old man stared at the ceiling. "You watch your indicator. It rings a little bell each time it rides across the screw. Then I got my marks on the cable, too. I know where that bucket is any time, right to the foot."

"How far to the bottom level?"

"In winter she varies against the summer stretch, but you can adjust for that. Don't you worry none, boy. I know where that bucket stands all the time. I've never hurt a man." Stanfield closed his eyes.

"How far to the bottom level?"

With his eyes still closed, Stanfield spoke with the clarity of great age for far yesterdays. "Twenty-two hundred and forty-five feet."

"How far up to the next level?"

"Seventy-five, on the cable. Most of the levels, except the third and seventh . . . but down deep. . . ." The old man's voice whispered away. His mouth fell open and he slept.

"I think you'd better go now," the matron said. "Maybe tomorrow, or some other time. . . ."

"I have to know one more thing." Cannon and the matron looked at each other gravely, both knowing there might never be another time, not even tomorrow.

Stanfield muttered irritably at the efforts to rouse him. At last he opened his eyes.

"Do you mean cable from the shaft house to the bottom, or from the surface to the bottom?" Cannon asked.

"Bottom of what?"

"The Wolf shaft." Cannon repeated his question.

"Collar measurement," Stanfield muttered. "We always figure. . . ." He drifted off again, his breathing light and rapid.

There seemed to be something indecent about stripping information from him and then walking out. Cannon hesitated. Once more Stanfield reminded him of the surface Wolf, desolate, forgotten, sinking away. Tonight, tomorrow—any moment.

"Is there anything he needs, anything he wants?" Linda asked.

The matron shook her head, smiling gently.

At noon the next day Cannon left Linda in Panlap and went on to the tunnel. He saw day shift men playing poker in the bunkhouse. The big compressors were idling.

Shipkey turned the Wolf maps slowly and said nothing while Cannon told his story to Gibson.

"We'll intersect the line of the Wolf bottom level at twenty-two hundred and six feet," the engineer said, "center point of our bore. We'll have thirty-one feet under the floor and twenty feet of good rock overhead. We can go right between the two levels!"

Shipkey said: "Those figures spill easy. Damn that kind of engineering. You'd risk men and hundreds of thousands of dollars on the guess work of a dying man."

"Stanfield wasn't guessing," Cannon said. "He knew those figures as well as you know your name, Brutus."

"Suppose there's a stope above the bottom level? What about a raise? You could run square into a raise connecting the two levels." Shipkey shook his head.

"Detwiler and Robey said there was no stope and no raise." Gibson was ready to fight.

"A guess from fifty years of forgetting," Shipkey said. "That's no way to drive a tunnel. I can put deep holes out and let the shaft drain, or I can back off and go clear around the Wolf."

"We can't!" Gibson said. "You let us get our tails in a

crack very neatly, didn't you?"

The tough old eyes looked Cannon and Gibson over insolently.

"Sure," Shipkey said.

They rallied to start hammering Shipkey again, to challenge him with violent words and noise. But, just in time, Cannon realized that would be another mistake. Old Brutus was watching them, waiting for their reaction.

"There's some risk, of course," Cannon said. "Me and Holy will take it, if you'll let us use the crews to drive in as close as we dare to the Wolf. How far are we now, Holy?"

"We're eighty feet away," Gibson said surlily. He had been set for a quarrel and it had not come.

Shipkey said: "You went a little farther than I told you to, Gibson."

"Three feet! My God, Shipkey. . . ." The engineer stopped suddenly. "Yeah, we went three feet farther than what you allowed us."

Now it was Shipkey who appeared irritated because an expected explosion had not materialized.

"You're too close to the Wolf now," he told the men.

"We're in good limestone," Cannon said. "We can shoot full rounds till we get close to the ore vein that's supposed to be in line with the Wolf levels. Then Holy and me will drive a pilot bore through."

Shipkey shook his head. "You're trusting maps that might be wrong. You're trusting hearsay from men. . . ."

"Look for yourself, Brutus." Gibson held the Wolf maps toward Shipkey. "Mike Stanfield said the third and seventh levels were farther apart than all the rest. What do the maps say?"

Stanfield had not said precisely that, but he had said the third and seventh levels were different from all the rest.

"I checked that when Cannon told the story," Shipkey said. "Stanfield was right there, but that doesn't mean. . . ."

"It's evidence that he knew what he was talking about," Gibson said.

He and Cannon had gathered all the evidence they had to support their plan. They took turns punching it into Shipkey, premise by premise, fact by fact. He knew as well as they that some of it was solid, that the whole of it was tricky, but it seemed to Cannon that he was more interested in their attitude than in their arguments.

This time, instead of anger, they threw logic at him, working as a team. Shipkey listened, weighing them coolly.

Linda's car came off the hill and stopped beside the office. She did not come inside immediately.

"You're not young any more, Brutus," Cannon said, "but suppose somebody drove you out of tunnel work. It would kill you. You're forcing us to retire before we even have a chance . . . if you don't let us go through the Wolf."

"Kid talk," Shipkey said. "You can go build roads or piddle around with building excavation."

Gibson said: "We've learned our lesson."

"Have you?" The old man gave the engineer a long glance. "You've learned that you can't ride over me. You're tried for safety on the Panlap, but I forced that. Have you learned anything that will bring back the scaler you killed?"

That was damned unfair, Cannon thought—they had suffered enough for an accident that might have happened under any circumstances. He was afraid that Gibson would lose his temper, but the engineer said nothing. Gibson would take anything right now for a chance to finish the Panlap.

Linda walked into a silent room. She did not speak and no one spoke to her. She stopped near Cannon's desk. Her father looked from her to Cannon slowly, and his tough old eyes were unreadable.

Cannon met the old man's stare. "Everything's said. What is it, Brutus?"

Shipkey let the silence hold a while. "No."

It battered deep into Cannon, past anger and regret. *No.* It was a brutal word, a thought that should not be accepted. But in the end, he had to accept it because that was all there was. Cannon and Gibson were done.

"That's lousy, Brutus," Linda said.

"Shut up!" The old man stared at her.

"Satisfied, Cannon?" Shipkey asked.

"Hell, no, I'm not."

Gibson's face was white. He turned away, looking from a window.

"What about you, Gibson?" Shipkey asked.

"It's your turn now," the engineer said curtly. He turned to say more, and then he let it go.

"That's it, then," Shipkey said. "You two pups are learning. When you can get bit across the face by a cold-blooded no and keep your mouths shut because there's nothing else for you to do, you're starting to learn." He walked to the door. "Go ahead and put the tunnel through the Wolf, if you think you're men enough."

They stood at the switch two thousand feet from the heading. The last heavy round had been shot and mucked away. The bulldog, the mucker, and all the other expensive equipment had been taken to daylight and pulled around a shoulder of the hill at the portal. Cannon and Gibson were alone in the Panlap now, alone with the water, the Tommy-knockers, and the sleeping Wolf.

Cannon pulled the switch, closing the circuit on primers

nested in mashed dynamite in the shallow holes he and Gibson had drilled with jackhammers. The sound was a roaring shock as the electrically timed charges went so close together they made just one tremendous blast.

Their clothing rattled as the concussion waves shot past. The airlines sang a thin metallic sound. Weird rings of light chased each other down the bore. When the sounds had washed away toward daylight, the noise of the water seemed much louder than before.

It was water they were thinking of.

Gibson picked up the phone. "All right, so far."

It made Cannon feel a little better to see the engineer's hands trembling.

They sloshed back to the heading through water that was overflowing the track. The exhaust fans were pulling, but the sweetish fumes of dynamite came drifting from the shattered rock. From a small station they carried up their gear, the jackhammers, air hoses, floodlights, everything they needed.

Their round had just outlined the small pioneer bore they would drive through the Wolf, perhaps. They mucked back waste to drill again, leaving it to pile up in the big bore.

The floodlights gleamed on the endless bursting of water from ancient seams two thousand feet down in the earth. The odor was nauseous, iron rust, water-rotted timber, old dynamite fumes that cling forever in abandoned mines, and slime and desolation. The terrible pressure of the great water column of the Wolf was squeezing débris through seams the eye could scarcely see. There was an odor of fear, also, which Cannon and Gibson did not attempt to hide from each other.

The jackhammers, tiny tools for tunnel work, awkward

tools, grew heavier after each round. The icy, stinking water kept splashing down. Sometime, deep in the night, fighting the rock grimly, Cannon thought he saw the whole face bulging out at him like a rotten sock. He cut his air before he could restrain himself.

Gibson shut down his drill. His voice was sharp. "What's the matter?"

"Nothing." Cannon shook his head. They were right, he was sure, but they really did not know. There might be open ground or weakened ground within a few feet of them. Any round might smash a thin barrier between them and the Wolf. The dirty water ran, and the rock seemed to move.

"How far are we from the vein?" Cannon asked. His voice came hollowly out of the dark behind him, out of the unknown ahead.

"This round or the next," Gibson said. "It depends on how wide the vein is. Robey and Detwiler said five feet."

Mike Stanfield had given figures too, dredging them from the deep yesterdays. Cannon thought wearily that he himself could not remember events of three days before. In his tired brain the rock kept pulsing out at him like a diaphragm that would strain so far before it broke.

Their next shots opened up a shining wall of lead-zinc ore, with the water curling down it steadily. They were tickling the very guts of the Wolf now. It was this vein that miners had followed two thousand feet down into water that stood knee level all the time in spite of everything the best pumps in the world could do. Above and below them there was open ground. Their margin of clearance, strong when hurled at Brutus Shipkey, shrank tightly around them now. Their imaginations could see clearly through the limestone to black water waiting.

Cold and wet, more scared than when Brutus Shipkey took them into their first tunnel, they drilled into the ore. They did not hear Shipkey, when he walked up behind them. Cannon's whole nervous system jerked when he saw the black-garbed figure standing in the gloom behind the floodlights.

Shipkey stayed there, silent, unmoving, until the round was in. He said casually: "Sounds solid enough, although cold water can send back a hard sound, too."

Something in his voice took Cannon back to the days when they were learning from him, before they began to know more of tunnel work than he did. Cannon could not see the old man clearly, but his words and a feeling that came from his being here said that one part of the fight was over.

Shipkey had beaten his lesson in; he would never again mention a scaler who had died in the Kokomo. That being so, Cannon and Gibson would never forget.

They began to coil the air hoses, staggering and slipping in the water that lay trapped by the muck pile. Cannon said: "You'd better get out of here, Brutus. We're not through yet."

Shipkey's smile was a brief flash of white, seen through the water splashing past his face. He started walking out. He was gone when they discovered the gallon jug of coffee.

"We're in again," Gibson said.

"Yeah. He'll make it tough again, too, when we slip a little."

Gibson simply grunted.

Sometime during the morning they drove through the last of a six-foot streak of ore and into granite on the footwall of the vein. They were past the Wolf.

Others could enlarge the pioneer bore to the tunnel dimensions, timber it solidly, move on ahead slowly with shallow rounds until the bore was safely clear of this area that hung between two levels of the Wolf.

They stumbled back to the firing station. Cannon picked up the phone. "She's through. She's holding. Tell. . . ."

"Stay out of the way," Shipkey answered. "Stuff is coming in." Not long afterward they heard the rumble of the bulldog hauling heavy traffic.

Shipkey stopped at the station briefly. There was a job ahead and he would be there to see that it was done well.

"You got anything to brag about?" he asked.

They looked at him warily. Cannon said: "Thanks for the coffee."

The old man climbed into a muck car and signaled Silent Anderson to take the mucker in. "You may make tunnel men someday," Shipkey said. "You're starting to learn."

The mucking machine went grinding up the rails.

"That's all we dare thank him for on this job," Gibson said.

Linda was waiting in the office when Cannon went in. She looked as cool and expensive as ever, but Cannon knew it was not so; he could afford to change his mind now.

"You're filthy," she said.

"Don't try to act like your old man."

"Do you think you're a big-shot tunnel man now?"

Cannon grinned. "Between you and me, yes."

Tanglefoot Goes to War

The fat cow buffalo went galumphing away in fright when Tanglefoot crashed out of the trees. He should not have appeared until ten minutes later, and then with the ponies, but there he was and there went the cow.

In the little park below, Sun Dog and Pawing Buffalo lay in the tall grass. They felt slightly murderous. After making the finest belly crawl of their lives for almost a half mile, they had been just a fraction short of effective arrow range.

Soon they would have had fat meat to fill their empty bellies, but all that they now had were burrs under their breechclouts.

"Too bad!" Tanglefoot called. "That's the way it goes sometimes." Wrinkles broke across his wide Ute forehead in a storm as he tried to remember something that had been troubling him all morning.

His parents had named him Gentle-Dew-On-The-Morning-Grass-In-The-Moon-Of-Bursting-Leaves. That didn't stick very long. When he was three, everybody began to call him Tanglefoot. He was a splendid-looking specimen of the People. When he was nine, a raiding party of Arapahoes had spied him watching ponies, and such a promising-looking lad he was that the Arapahoes spent three days working out a plan to capture him.

They captured him. Two days later they brought him back.

Suddenly Tanglefoot recalled what it was that was bothering him. Rocks in his moccasin. He'd been walking on them all morning. Back a piece in the thicket he saw a dead aspen slanting out from a tangle of fallen trees, an ideal place to sit in comfort while he removed the moccasin.

Down on Famine Flats, Pawing Buffalo raked the worst of the burrs from his underside. He shook his head in a disgusted sort of way and lay right where he was. Wide and fat was Pawing Buffalo. He nestled down into the grass. Let nature take its course. If he couldn't eat, he'd just as well sleep. Only he was too hungry to sleep. *A-i-e-e,* that had been a fine buffalo cow.

All the time they had been sneaking up on it, Pawing Buffalo had seen it not as a big woolly brute munching grass but as hump ribs and boss and fleece fat and other stuff too delectable to mention. His stomach rumbled in sympathy. Why had Tanglefoot ever been born? Oh, why?

All at once Sun Dog stopped grinding his teeth and touched Pawing Buffalo's back lightly in a warning gesture. The lean and wiry Sun Dog, hunter, warrior, *bon vivant,* and chaser of Ute maidens, was peering intently through the gently waving top of the grass. He eased down silently and made quick signs.

Antelope, five of them, were coming downwind into the park. Antelope from the west. It was a good omen. "Make ready with your arrows, Pawing Buffalo, and, when I give the word, we will spring up and fire."

Pawing Buffalo was all ears. Meat on the fire!

Soon they could hear the antelope, the soft touch of tiny

hoofs, the whisper of grass against trim legs as the fleet ones came closer, unsuspecting. Pawing Buffalo knew well the old Ute saying about making rabbit stew after catching the rabbit, and he knew, too, what an antelope looked like with the hair on, but his mind reduced the non-essentials right down to the nub.

His mind ran red with a vision of meat roasting in great chunks.

Closer now the fleet ones. A buck made a soft blowing noise. Sun Dog's eyes were pinched down, gleaming like wet, black stone. Wait, wait, he signaled, they're going to come right to us.

And so it seemed.

The sound of a breaking tree came from the hill like a clap of thunder in bright sunshine. Sun Dog and Pawing Buffalo leaped up with arrows on the string, but the antelope had not come close enough and now they were skimming away. The hunters drew a blank. They tried, but the narrow rumps of fleeing antelope are narrow, indeed, at extended range.

Before Pawing Buffalo completed his first groan, meat on the fire became meat that twinkled over the hills and far away.

In the aspens, Tanglefoot scrooched away from the treacherous pole that had broken when he started to sit down. He removed his moccasin and spilled out a handful of pebbles and assorted twig ends, and then he regarded the moccasin with solemn awe. When it was off his foot, it certainly had a big look about it.

Perhaps his companions had heard the crash; they might be worried about him. Carrying his moccasin, Tanglefoot stepped from the trees once more to reassure his brothers. His bare foot brushed a cactus and caused him to let out a great howl as he hopped about, but then he observed that only a few spines were sticking, so, as he extracted them, he called down happily: "I am not greatly injured. Do not worry."

It was strange the way Pawing Buffalo and Sun Dog stared up at him. They were saying something, but Tanglefoot could not hear what it was.

"I will lead you to game," Tanglefoot said.

In a choked voice, Sun Dog asked: "Where are the ponies?"

"They are safe," Tanglefoot replied. "I will get them."

As he walked away, at last remembering to put on his moccasin, his brothers waited to hear another tremendous crashing noise. None came. Of course, there was no game in sight. Slowly Sun Dog sank to the ground. He lay on his stomach and beat his head against the sod and he made odd noises through clenched teeth.

Pawing Buffalo sat down. "I am hungry."

"Death to him!" Sun Dog said. "We have suffered too long. When he returns, we will kill him!"

"Our boyhood chum?"

"Him!"

Pawing Buffalo was perturbed. "There's Ute law about such things, you know."

"Squaw law, Tanglefoot has got to go!"

Pawing Buffalo's stomach rumbled. "I don't know, Sun Dog. He's always been that way and. . . ."

"Death to him! He's messed us up too often."

"True," Pawing Buffalo said. His stomach rumbled again.

"First a fat buffalo, then the antelope. What do we do . . . wait until he gets us killed by the Arapahoes?"

"I'm not worried about that." The thought of meat,

however, gave Pawing Buffalo a pained expression. "It should be done by council."

"We will be the council!"

Pawing Buffalo was still doubtful, but when they rose and walked toward the hill, he saw the tracks of the buffalo cow. How deeply she had sunk into the soft earth near a wallow. How fat she must have been. His stomach growled assent. "Perhaps you are right, Sun Dog."

They met Tanglefoot coming through the trees.

He said: "I have something to tell you. It seems. . . ."

"Sit down, lout," Sun Dog said. "We have something more important to tell you."

"But. . . ."

"Sit down!" Sun Dog drew his knife.

Tanglefoot sighed and sat. What was it with them, anyway?

"It's like this," Sun Dog said, "you've got to go."

"Me? I can't. You see. . . ."

"We've got to kill you, Tanglefoot."

Tanglefoot blinked at Pawing Buffalo. "You, too?"

"I'm afraid so."

"Over one measly buffalo cow?"

"Over a thousand buffalo, a million antelope, more than twenty years of foul-ups!" Sun Dog cried.

Tanglefoot relaxed with his back to a tree. He looked miserable. "I guess you're right. I try, but everything goes wrong."

"Maybe . . . ," Pawing Buffalo started to suggest something.

"Maybe nothing!" Sun Dog yelled. "I don't want none of your remember-when-we-were-kids-together stuff, or how he saved my life when he dropped on the Arapaho chief, Big Mouth, that time when I was almost done. He fell out of that tree on Big Mouth by accident, in the first place. He was supposed to be on the other side of the rocks. . . . Why am I going into all this?" Sun Dog glared down at Tanglefoot. "You're going to die."

"Who does it?" Pawing Buffalo asked. "Not me. I remember when. . . ."

"Never mind remembering! We'll both do it. We'll put our war ropes on him and drag him to death with our ponies."

Pawing Buffalo stared gloomily at the earth. He was so hungry he couldn't think up a defense for Tanglefoot.

"Have you anything to say?" Sun Dog asked Tanglefoot.

"You can't kill me like that."

"Hah! And why not?"

"No ponies to drag me behind," Tanglefoot said. "Two Arapahoes stole them while we were stalking the buffalo. That's what I was trying to tell you a minute ago. But I have a plan to get them back. Now listen carefully. . . ."

Whatever the plan was, nobody but Tanglefoot heard it. Sun Dog's belligerence departed with a *whoosh*. He bowed his head and began to bump it against a tree, and there he stood in helpless frustration, a warrior so close to tears that it was painful to look upon him.

Pawing Buffalo sat down and put his arms across his stomach, where most of his emotions lay. He rocked back and forth as if in deep thought.

Tanglefoot rattled on, but his brothers did not hear, and, when they at last looked at each other, they were in agreement. It would do no good to kill Tanglefoot; his spirit would return to break their bows and scare their ponies and kick dirt on their cooking meat and mess things up just as much as the real Tanglefoot.

When he was alive, they could at least get some satisfaction from threatening to kill him, and they could always hit him a solid lick across the rump now and then with their bows, but nobody ever had any luck connecting with a swing at a spirit.

"Had I suspected Arapahoes were about, of course, I would have been more careful with the ponies," Tanglefoot was saying, "but, no matter, I will lead you in recovering the ponies and no doubt we will kill a few Araps in the bargain. Follow me, my brothers!"

Numbly Pawing Buffalo and Sun Dog rose and followed Tanglefoot.

"I think it was Arapahoes that got the ponies," Tanglefoot said. "You know, of course, I do occasionally make small mistakes in reading sign."

Small mistakes, indeed, Sun Dog thought wearily; it was probably the ponies that had captured the Arapahoes.

Two sleeps back to camp, Pawing Buffalo was thinking. Two sleeps, that was, by pony. Now they were on foot, and hunger was destroying him.

Just then Tanglefoot brushed past a springy branch and bent it forward. Instead of holding it and easing it back, he passed on. The branch came whipping back and slapped Pawing Buffalo a stinging blow on the upper lip. *"Wagh!"* he grunted.

"Courage," Sun Dog said. "Maybe the Arapahoes will capture us and torture us to death, and then we will be free of him!"

When there was no way for the band to prevent it, Pawing Buffalo, Sun Dog, and Tanglefoot made their home with a group of brother Uncompaghres under the leadership of His-Weight-Makes-The-Spotted-Pony-Sag-And-Grunt. The chief preferred to be called Spotted Pony, but he had certain fitting attributes that caused him to be referred to commonly as Sag And Grunt.

All was serene in his camp at the moment. Most of the young men were out hunting or bumming around the hills somewhere, his wife was cooking up a walloping fine buffalo stew, and Fair-Wind-Caressing-A-Shaft-Of-Sunlight was in good view a short distance away, working on a winter lodge.

Sag And Grunt smoked his pipe and watched Fair Wind. Arapaho, she was, captured when she was eight. She was the daughter of old Chief Big Mouth himself, the Utes' most hated enemy. Now it was time for her to marry, but it was going to take a heap of ponies to deal with her foster parents. Just how many?

Sag And Grunt glanced at his wife, Waddles-Through-The-Willows-When-The-Bloom-Is-On-The-Sage. *Ugh!* She was getting to be quite a slob. He sniffed the odor of her stew with vast approval, but his eyes went back to Fair Wind. Fifteen ponies, maybe?

He-Rides-Like-A-Sack-Of-Wet-Buckskin came into camp all a-lather. *"Yikes!"* he whooped. "The enemy is here!"

Sag And Grunt rose with dignity. "Quit making such a show of yourself. You mean Tanglefoot is back?"

He Rides whipped his pony around the camp, shouting: "The Striped Arrow People!! To arms! Arapahoes! *Wagh!*"

Women wailed and grabbed their children. Dogs barked and bit each other. The few warriors left in camp ran about bumping into things. Sag And Grunt at last hammered some order into affairs, enough to get a proper report from He Rides.

The enemy was across the river, not a mile way, a strong raiding party, although not in numbers like the leaves of the trees, as He Rides first said. Sag And Grunt sent two scouts to throw a study on things. He-Scoots-Through-The-Brush and the veteran, Doesn't-Pop-The-Twigs-Much-That-Is.

An hour later the scouts returned with a fairly accurate report. About twenty of the enemy encamped at Hot Rocks Springs, with old Big Mouth himself there in person. Pretty sneaky. The Araps had an invulnerable position in the rocks, with a plain in front of them and open ground behind them.

Even if he had all his fighting men present, Sag And Grunt wouldn't have enough to make a surround.

Little-Beaver-Calling-His-Mate said: "Lead us, Sag And Grunt, and we will charge in among them, few though we are, and carve the living daylights out of them hand to hand." Little Beaver was young. He'd listened too much to his elders telling lies around the fire at nights.

Sag And Grunt gave him a sour look and made a note to instruct Little Beaver privately about the merits of hand-to-hand combat. A man could get killed that way.

The chief sent two men to round up all the hunters as soon as possible. As any Indian knew, the first thing you ought to have was a three-to-one bulge in numbers when it came to fighting. Then Sag And Grunt told the women to shut up, and the boys to watch the pony herd closely, and the old men to stir around a bit and make a show of numbers. This done, the chief rode out with He Scoots and Doesn't Pop and one or two others to look the situation over.

He knew those rocks across the river well. There was forage there, and water, and, no doubt, the Arapahoes had brought plenty of dried meat. They would hang around and embarrass him as long as possible. He rode up to the high bank above the Shining River and howled a few insults across at the rocks.

Chief Big Mouth came from the rocks on his pinto. Gadfrey, but he was a repulsive-looking Indian by any Ute standard you cared to apply. Back and forth on opposite sides of the river the two chiefs rode, telling each other unkind things. Now and then they arched a high shot just to prove that their bows were in working order and that they disliked each other. They raced at full speed to pick up each other's spent arrows. This went on for some time, and honor was served.

When they were reduced to yelling such low insults at each other as—"Yah, yah, yah, you couldn't catch a flea!"— they broke off the engagement by mutual consent.

On his way back to camp, Sag And Grunt mulled over the ideas he'd picked up from studying the land. When his hunters returned, he'd have about two to one on Big Mouth. Not much, but with a little strategy he would make those Araps wish they'd never entered the mountains, and he would cover himself with glory.

He set a tight watch, and then he went into council with himself. A whacking victory over Big Mouth's bunch would really fix things up. How could Fair Wind's foster parents hold out against a chief who had just knocked the stuffings out of the Arapahoes? Ten ponies? Make it five.

The Ute hunters began to straggle in at dusk, and with them came about twenty warriors of the Cochetopa band, who had been camped only ten miles away. A good many family quarrels ensued, for some of the wives of the Uncompaghres wanted to know if their husbands had been hunting or horsing around in the camp of their cousins for two days.

You've no idea how suspicious some of those wives were.

"Knock it off!" Sag And Grunt yelled. "We've got trouble enough. Now hear my plan."

Scratches-His-Back-With-A-Pine-Cone-Tied-To-A-Stick was a grizzled old fighter, veteran of many a combat with the Arapahoes. To Sometimes-Catches-An-Antelope he muttered: "His plan! He's always planning and we generally wind up with our tails in a crack. You'd think Tanglefoot himself was his adviser. Where is Tanglefoot, by the way?"

"Far away," Sometimes Catches said. "Fortunately."

"First, we got to lure them Araps out of the rocks," Sag And Grunt said.

"Who bells the cat?" Scratches inquired. Sometimes he got a little tired of war. In thirty years of fighting he'd killed only two Arapahoes, and nearly been killed a dozen times. For such meager results he'd attended 1,000 councils, ridden 10,000 miles, and shot off enough arrows to build a large beaver dam. Sometimes he wondered if the earth would open, and the mountains would crumble away in dust, and all the leaves fall from the trembling trees in mid-summer if the Utes and Arapahoes forgot their troubles and tried to live like gentlemen. Quite likely nothing at all would happen. Scratches was too wise, however, to voice such traitorous thoughts.

"First we got to lure them out," Sag And Grunt said.

"You already said that," Sometimes Catches complained.

"Shut up and let me talk." The chief scowled. "Just yelling insults won't work. In the first place, it's awful hard to insult an Arap. What we need is some kind of prize to make them drool, something to make them risk their necks."

"Ponies!" said Doesn't Pop.

Everybody considered that thought, especially Sag And Grunt, who happened to have more ponies than anyone else. He didn't like some of the sly looks he saw being exchanged around the fire.

"Sag And Grunt is wise," Scratches said. He tapped his head. "He thinks well. Twenty ponies placed in easy reach of the enemy, with our men in ambush. . . ."

"Whose ponies are you talking about?" the chief demanded.

Everyone shrugged and looked at each other as if to say such a question was unnecessary. It was well known that chiefs should be generous, brave, and wise—and also supply the ponies to bait a trap when the general welfare of the People was involved.

"Now just a minute here!" Sag And Grunt said.

"An excellent lure to draw them out," Scratches said. "Thirty ponies would be better, and then with the plan you have in mind. . . . What is the plan, wise one?"

"Not so fast, not so fast." Sag And Grunt glared at the smirking scoundrels. In the background the women were standing quietly and listening. Fair Wind was there, tall and calm.

Sag And Grunt proceeded to get off the hook. "It's obvious that old Big Mouth has come into our country to try to steal his daughter. Instead of ponies, we'll bait the trap with Fair Wind."

There was merit in that thought, sure enough. The Utes grunted approval. They didn't dare to worry about Fair Wind's double-crossing them; she'd been raised as a Ute, and for all she cared the Arapahoes and Big Mouth were only names.

"We still ought to have about fifteen ponies to make things sure-fire," Scratches said.

Try as he might, Sag And Grunt couldn't get away from that disgusting idea. *The lousy chisellers!* "All right," he growled. "I'll put up ten ponies!"

"Good ones, none of those crow-baits you've been trying the palm off for the last two seasons," Scratches said. "We want to be sure to get the Araps all excited, don't we, boys?"

The boys were quick to agree. "Yup, yup!" they said.

Sag And Grunt made a note to give Waddles the dickens for inviting Scratches to chow every time he looked hungry.

Far across the Shining River came the faint, shrill sounds of the Arapahoes having some kind of outlandish war dance. The heathens.

"Now, wise one," Scratches said smugly, "the rest of your plan."

Make sure you're going to be right in the first line, you ape, Sag And Grunt thought. But he composed his face and looked real chiefly, as a good chief should. "Hear me, my people. . . ."

It would take some doings, old Sag And Grunt's idea. It called for a division of forces, one group to conceal themselves in the willows on the Ute side of the river, facing the ford where the enemy would have to cross when they came after Fair Wind and the ponies. Since the position had to be gained by night and by wading the icy waters of the Shining River for a mile or so in order not to leave tracks, everyone maintained a sort of dark silence about who should have the honor.

Sag And Grunt tried to hand this business to the Cochetopas, speaking of the glory that would come from it. But the Cochetopas, like any other Utes, were not enthusiastic about roaming around at night in a river.

Big-Windy-From-The-Cañon, leader of the Cochetopas, declined the honor with thanks. He said his boys were more qualified to take the second detail, which called for going far down the river, then swinging back while riding, not walking, in the water, thence up the steep bank in single file to gain a position in some rocks somewhat downriver but on the same side of the stream as the Arapaho camp.

There this detail would stay concealed until the enemy was drawn out far enough so that Big Windy's boys could sweep in between the Araps and their rock stronghold. That phase achieved, what with the Utes in the willows completely discombooberating the enemy when he tried to cross the river, the thing ought to turn into a buffalo hunt.

It was a most excellent armchair plan.

"Now let me brief you again," Sag And Grunt said. "They'll be drawn out when they see Fair Wind and my five ponies across the river. . . ."

"Ten ponies," Scratches corrected. "Good ones, remember!"

Sag And Grunt ignored him. "Some of these heathens know who Fair Wind is. They'll recognize her. Sure, they'll be a mite suspicious at first. They may even probe the willows with casual fire. . . ."

"What do you call casual fire?" Seldom-Leaves-The-Lodge inquired quickly. He was on the willow detail.

"Oh, light skirmish stuff." Sag And Grunt waved it off with his hand. "A few arrows here and there, maybe a blast or so from some of those old fusils they have. They're miserable shots. To make it look good, three of you will scamper up the bank and retreat as far as where Fair Wind is holding the ponies."

"I volunteer for that," Seldom Leaves said. "I'll make it look awful good."

"No doubt," the chief said sourly. "Only three, mind you. The rest stay low and stand firm. We don't return the fire. The Araps will think they've flushed out three scouts. When the main body of them is in the river, we give them blazes. They retreat, but, by then, Big Windy and his boys will be cutting in behind them. The Araps will have no place to fall back on. We'll rack 'em up all over the joint."

"Yeah," Scratches said. He was all scarred up from having participated in countless rack-'em-up campaigns against the Arapahoes. What would happen if they followed Little Beaver's childish thought and went barreling into the rocks to meet the enemy tooth and toenail? He knew: A heap of Indians would get clobbered up and the principles of warfare would be set back one thousand years. No, you had to follow the book.

Everybody took a good check on the Dog Star, although some couldn't read a lick of time from it no matter how they tried. Then the two parties set forth.

Sag And Grunt led the willow party. Upstream they went for two miles, then into the river. It was bitter cold and the rocks were big and slippery. Little Beaver fell into a deep hole and came up gasping. All the glory of war faded for him and he tried to sneak along the bank where the going was easier, but Scratches shoved him back into the water.

Soon after Scratches rapped his bad knee against a rock. "May the sky fall!" he grunted. He hobbled along, thinking of his kill average against the Araps. One every fifteen years. What a miserable way to make a living. When he was young, his uncle, Shakes-Up-A-Few-Tricks, had pleaded with him to go into the medicine man end of the business, but, no, Scratches had to be a warrior.

It was a terrible trip, slopping along in the water, falling over rocks. Seldom Leaves got carried away by a strong current and became all wrapped up in the branches of a cottonwood that had fallen into the river. When the others dragged him free, the limbs stripped away his breechclout and moccasins. A fine show he was going to make when it came time to retreat from the casual fire.

It was the most shivering, barked-shin group of bedraggled Utes as you may ever see that finally wound up in the willows at the ambush spot. Swampy ground, complete with mosquitoes. There they huddled in gallant ambush, some of them muttering unkind things about Sag And Grunt.

"Tanglefoot himself might have thought this one up," Scoots growled.

The Cochetopas weren't having any ball, either. Jumps-At-Shadows was thrown from his pony when it slipped and fell. He was knocked colder than a wet moccasin. They tied him across his horse and went on. When it came time to go up the bank, Big Windy couldn't find the place Sag And Grunt had talked about.

Big Windy finally chose a place where the ascent was so steep that the warriors had to boost the ponies. He sat down and gasped for a while, wondering if an Arap scalp was worth it, even if you could get one.

They tried the bank again, forgetting that Jumps was only loosely tied to his pony. He slid off and fell on top of Fish Catcher, who was boosting. The collision knocked Fish Catcher cold but it helped revive Jumps, who came out of it with a start, thinking he was surrounded by enemies. He put up a good fight until they knocked him cold once more.

"By all the wise beavers of the Shagg River, how did we ever get into this mess?" someone asked plaintively.

"Isn't old Sag's bunch the one that Tanglefoot belongs to?" another warrior inquired.

"Yeah," Big Windy said, and that was a sort of explanation of all their woes. He sent a man to scout the rocks where they were going to hide, figuring that the Araps were sneaky enough to have placed an outpost there.

All was clear. There was nothing to it now but wait out the night, shed the morning dew from their bare hides, and ride out to glorious victory when the time came.

At daylight Big Windy's boys could see the Arap lookouts sprawled around on the rocks farther upriver. The Ute camp came to life. Two young boys rode out with Fair Wind when she took the ponies to graze. After a time Waddles brought out ten more ponies, leaving them with Fair Wind.

Big Windy grinned. That Waddles had all her marbles. If any of her old man's ponies were going to be snatched by the Araps, she was making sure that Sag And Grunt would lose enough to crimp any big deal he might want to make for a new, young wife.

Fair Wind played it smart. She didn't rush the decoy business by coming into snatching range of the Araps too quickly. She made it look natural as she let the herd drift closer to the river.

The sight of those Ute ponies began to work on the Arapahoes. Most of them came out of the rocks a short distance to have a better look. Big Mouth and four warriors rode over to the riverbank to size things up.

Big Mouth hadn't lived as long as he had by being a sucker for a pleasant-looking set-up. He pointed down at the willows on the far bank, and it was clear that he was telling his men: "Now there's a likely place to get into trouble."

He seemed to be urging one of his boys to go across and check out the willows, but the warrior was not about to do any such thing. He liked it up on the bank well enough.

Big Mouth studied the willows, the ponies, and the Ute camp, where old men and boys were riding around, raising a heap of dust, and yelling as if they were warriors getting up steam. From a distance, it appeared that all the Ute fighting men actually might be at their camp. Certainly the Arapaho chief had no way of knowing that twenty Cochetopas had reinforced the Uncompaghres. He did not make any hasty moves, just the same.

Fair Wind drifted a bit closer with the ponies. One of the Araps recognized her, and then things began to pick up. Big Mouth got all excited. He rode back and forth along the bank, calling for her to come over and join him, her true, ever-loving father. "Leave the Ute dogs!" he shouted. Then he added: "And bring the ponies!"

Fair Wind might not have heard. She withdrew a little, as if realizing that she was in danger. This excited the Araps all the more, the idea of those choice ponies getting farther away. Big Mouth's men came out from the rocks, urging a quick sortie to grab the loot.

Big Windy motioned for his boys to make ready. Once the Araps went down that high bank and started across, they wouldn't have a chance to get back before the Cochetopas cut them off. Maybe Sag And Grunt's plan was going to pay off, after all.

Fair Wind moved the ponies farther away. The Araps couldn't stand it, but Big Mouth held them back long enough to direct a plunging, probing fire into the willows across the way.

Down there in the swampy ground, all lumpy with mosquito bites, the Utes clawed in as arrows came whacking through the brush. Some of the enemy had muskets, loaded it seemed with scraps of broken kettles, the way stuff whizzed around.

"*A-i-e-e,*" Seldom Leaves moaned. So this was what Sag And Grunt called casual fire. He was being destroyed. Everybody was being destroyed. Seldom Leaves got up and hit for home, lack of moccasins, breechclout, and all. With him went the two others designated to retreat.

The Araps jeered and howled with scorn as they saw the trio of Utes sprinting away.

It worked, just as Sag And Grunt had said. The enemy mounted up and made ready to cross. The Uncompaghres made ready to receive them. Big Windy's boys stood by their ponies, itching to sally out.

Still on the trail of their ponies, a trail that led straight to the Arapaho camp, Tanglefoot and his two companions had observed part of the morning's activities from the hills beyond the camp. Things looked terrible for the Utes.

"It's murder!" Tanglefoot said. "Fair Wind will be captured, the ponies lost, and maybe the camp will be wiped out."

Sun Dog had a better eye for things. Something was fishy about Fair Wind's being out there with the herd, and something wasn't quite right about all that dust in the Ute camp. He was about to speak his thoughts when they were snowed under by Tanglefoot's fast talk.

"We've got to work fast," Tanglefoot said. "No doubt there's a few ponies left somewhere around that Arap camp. We'll come in that back way and grab them. You, Pawing Buffalo, swing over to the left. I'll go to the right. In the confusion we'll all get through to warn the camp, and I'll save Fair Wind on the way."

"You got a hole in your head," Sun Dog growled, "if you think I'm going to ride straight through the middle of those plug-uglies."

"They'll split," Tanglefoot said. "Part of them will chase me and part will chase Pawing Buffalo. That'll leave a big hole for you to go through."

"More likely the big hole will be through me."

"Forward," Tanglefoot said. "Let us get the ponies."

That part was easy. The rear of the Arapaho camp was unguarded, since the Araps thought they had all the enemy in front of them. Tanglefoot and his companions secured three ponies, and Pawing Buffalo even had time to grab a bunch of antelope meat lying by a fire pit.

"Let us ride bravely," Tanglefoot said. "It is a good day to die."

"You and your platitudes. You should live so long," Sun Dog grumbled. "Pawing Buff, how you going to ride with your mouth full of meat?"

"No trouble. If I must die, I wish to die happy."

"Hang back a little, Sun Dog," Tanglefoot said. "Then go through when we make an opening."

The enemy had just started down the riverbank when Tanglefoot and Pawing Buffalo burst out of the rocks. Tanglefoot went to the right. A majestic picture he made, what with his feet swinging low and his elbows all a-jog. Pawing Buffalo rode with the haunch of meat in his right hand like an overgrown war club. Even at full tilt, he now and then managed to snatch a bite.

Left on the bank as holders of spare ponies were a few young Araps, first-mission characters. Since they were absorbed in watching their companions on the way to strike a blow, they did not at once see Pawing Buffalo and Tanglefoot whizzing around their flanks.

When the Arap pony holders did see them, they began to yell bloody murder. "Utes in the rear! Utes in the rear!" They didn't bother to say how many, being new at the business.

Big Mouth bellowed for his boys to halt. "That's what I figured all along, a trap!" Just before his men reached comfortable arrow range of the ambush, Big Mouth got them turned, and in a wild scramble the Arapahoes started back up the bank.

Sag And Grunt was fit to be tied. For a moment he'd been looking right down Big Mouth's throat with a splendid warhead arrow that bore the Arap chief's name. And now the fine trap was dashed. Sag And Grunt howled his frustration. He began to shoot arrows into the dust and confusion, hoping for the best.

His boys were firing away, but it was poor range and the enemy was making an infernal dust. A few of the Araps were stuck with arrows in exposed, tender spots, but the rack-'em-up prospects went to pot in a twinkling.

Quite naturally Sag And Grunt thought that the Cochetopas had charged from concealment too soon; you never could trust a Cochetopa to co-operate properly. Nuts to the whole snafu outfit!

Sun Dog held back, as instructed, and then, when his two companions were well on their way, he rode out to make his dash through the center. Suddenly the whole Arapaho nation came riding up the bank, smack in his way. *"Ee-yawp!"* he said, and treated the symptoms as they arose, which meant that he turned and headed for the hills in the straightest possible line.

Over on the left, Pawing Buffalo blundered straight into the Cochetopas hiding in the rocks. They had been about to charge, and then Big Windy had held them back when he realized that one jaw of the trap had snapped on air. But maybe there was still a chance to make a little surprise.

Not with Pawing Buffalo around. He brandished the antelope joint. "Arapahoes! Charge!"

"Where did this clown come from?" Big Windy groaned.

Pawing Buffalo grabbed a couple of bites from his war

club. "Murder the bums!" he shouted, his words somewhat muffled by the meat in his mouth. "Charge!" He made such a scene, wheeling his pony, exhorting the Cochetopas to fall upon the enemy, that the Araps caught on.

Big Mouth even made a note to mention the alertness of his pony holders in his next report, although the pony holders were the most surprised of all when twenty Utes at last rode out into the open.

The Cochetopas were trapped by the ritual of war; they had to make some kind of show, even if they no longer had any advantage. It was a noisy battle and very dusty. The two contending forces rode all over the plain, shooting arrows and yelling like mad, but always holding to a respectable distance.

Sag And Grunt's men, on foot, disgusted, had no desire to charge out of the willows to get tromped on by some Arap's pony. A few of them did sneak up the bank and take long-range shots. It was a standoff, no one seriously injured, honor served, and about time for a mid-morning snack, when the Arapahoes began to withdraw.

Tanglefoot, the master strategist, fared well galumphing up, and just then the cinch snapped and he went sprawling against the feet of Fair Wind's pony. He staggered up and caught his breath. "Arapahoes!" he croaked. "Ride for your life while I stave them off!"

He lunged into the herd to catch himself a fresh pony, making such a commotion that he got the whole bunch excited. The ponies began to run upriver, but, even so, Tanglefoot might have caught a horse if he hadn't tripped over an ant hill that some ants had left lying around.

Fair Wind and her two young helpers tried to turn Sag And Grunt's herd back toward camp. They were just about to get the job done when three Arapahoes, who had broken off the unrewarding exercise of war and sneaked across the river, came barreling in like painted demons. Fair Wind and the boys had to let the herd go and ride for camp. One of the lads slowed his pony enough to let Tanglefoot leap up behind him. That was a mistake, for Tanglefoot hadn't brushed all the ants off himself. When they began to sting the pony, it went into a frenzy of bucking.

Once more Tanglefoot wound up on the ground, running the last quarter mile to camp, where Waddles was standing with a smug expression as she watched the three Araps make off with Sag And Grunt's ponies.

The Battle of Shining River was finished.

In two noisy bunches the Utes came straggling back to camp. Some of the younger ones were claiming a great victory, since the Arapahoes were leaving the country, but among the older warriors a tremendous argument was brewing concerning what had happened.

They agreed on one point: something had gone haywire.

Sag And Grunt was furious over the loss of his ponies. Without success he tried to enlist a detail to go after them, but the Utes had enough exercise for one day. Then Sag And Grunt tried to take it out on Big Windy. "You fouled things up by charging too soon!"

"Me charge too soon! You let your men in the willows fire too soon. That's what ruined things, plus the fact that you didn't cut me in on all the details."

"What d'you mean?" Sag And Grunt howled.

"Those three men you sent around to hit the Arap camp from the rear. I know the angle. They were after ponies and loot, while my men had to lay low in the rocks like a bunch of lizards!"

"It wasn't no picnic in the willows!" old Sag And Grunt

yelled. "Hey! What's this about three men in the rear?"

"As if you didn't know," Big Windy sneered. "Here's one of them right here." He looked around for Pawing Buffalo, but Pawing Buffalo had gone after food.

"Three of them, huh?" Sag And Grunt began to feel his way toward some answers. He saw Tanglefoot standing near a lodge.

"Plus the fact that you let your men fire too soon when the Araps started across the river," Big Windy said. "The next time any Uncompaghre ropes me into a half-baked plan. . . ."

Sag And Grunt had started toward Tanglefoot, but now he turned. "You're saying I ruined everything? Any time you try to co-operate with a bunch of knot-headed Cochetopas. . . ."

It developed into an interesting discussion. Tanglefoot was saved temporarily, and it was then he was joined by Sun Dog, who was just arriving after making a wide circle to evade the Arapahoes. "You and your big hole in the center!" he growled. "I got a notion to. . . ."

"I have a better one," someone said, and that was Waddles. She had a large pouch of food. "You two had better pry Pawing Buffalo out of the cooking pot and go visit somewhere, maybe up in the White River country."

Sag And Grunt and Big Windy were still blistering each other something fierce, but it was not going to last forever, Sun Dog knew. He took the food and slipped away quickly to find Pawing Buffalo. Let Tanglefoot shift for himself.

Pawing Buffalo saw the wisdom of going somewhere. He and Sun Dog rode away. "Let it fall where it properly belongs, on Tanglefoot," Sun Dog said. "When the heat is off, we will return."

They were far away in a scrub oak thicket when they

spied the Cochetopas returning to their camp. The way they were riding, the sullen, angry look of them, told Pawing Buffalo and Sun Dog that it was best to let their brothers go without joining them.

The two Utes laid low until the Cochetopas were out of sight.

"Now what?" Pawing Buffalo inquired. "Waddles didn't give us too much food, you know."

"Without Tanglefoot it will be simple to kill game. Without Tanglefoot it will be possible to visit the camps of our brothers and not be thrown out." Sun Dog lay back for a brief rest. "Without Tanglefoot . . . ah!"

Not long after they resumed their way, they spied a fat brown bear in a patch of raspberries among the rocks. With great skill they stalked it, creeping below an intervening ridge so that they could pop up suddenly at close range.

They popped.

The bear was gone.

Tanglefoot was sitting on a bedraggled pony above the berry patch. "If you'd been a little sooner, you might have had a shot at a bear," he said. "Greetings, my brothers. I knew I could find you, although I was a little late getting started. Waddles seemed to think it best that I join you, although, for the life of me, I don't know yet what went wrong today."

Sun Dog leaned against a trembling tree. He knocked on it with his head, swaying back and forth with a helpless look upon his dark face.

"I would have shot that bear myself, but I forgot my bow," Tanglefoot said. "No matter. I can get another when we reach the White River. You two have never been there, have you?"

Numbly Pawing Buffalo shook his head.

"I will lead you," Tanglefoot said, "and it is best that we go now, since I noticed from about a half mile back that Sag And Grunt has sent a detail after us, the sorehead."

They left quickly.

"May the Great Spirit help our White River brothers," Pawing Buffalo said.

Nights of Terror

I

Young Bill Orahood, the Sky Hook owner, was waiting for Ken Baylor where the trail forked near the fall-dry bed of Little Teton Creek. Orahood was mostly arms and legs and a long neck. Without a word he swung his chunky sorrel in beside Baylor, and they rode toward Crowheart.

They went a quarter of a mile before Orahood blurted out the question that everyone in the Crowheart country was asking: "What do you suppose got Paxton?"

Baylor shook his head. Maybe Doc Raven knew by now. Raven had not been in town late yesterday afternoon when a drifting rider brought Bill Paxton's body out of Big Ghost Basin.

"You saw Paxton?" Orahood asked. "After. . . ."

"Yeah." It was something to forget, if a man could.

A mile from town they caught up with big Arn Kullhem. A wide chunk of a man, his flat jaw bristling with sandy stubble, Kullhem looked at them from deep-set eyes and did not even grunt when they spoke. His Double K lay right on the break into the Big Ghost. More than any rancher, he had suffered from what was happening down in the basin.

Bridle bits and saddle leather and hoofs against the autumn-crisp grass made the only sounds around them until they came to the top of the last rolling hill above Crowheart. Then Kullhem said: "Doc Haven didn't give us no help on them first two."

Bill Paxton was the third man to die in Big Ghost. First, an unknown rider, and then Perry Franks, Kullhem's foreman. Both Franks and Paxton, one of the twins of Crow Tracks, had staked out in the basin to get a line on the shadowy men who were wrecking the Crowheart ranchers. *If they had died from bullets,* Baylor thought, *the situation would be clear enough.*

"Who's going to stay down in the basin now?" Kullhem growled.

Orahood and Baylor looked at each other. Strain had been building higher on Orahood's blistered face the closer they rode to town. He and Baylor glanced over their shoulders at the hazed ridges that marked the break above the gloomy forests of Big Ghost. Up here the grass was good, but, when the creeks ran low, cattle went over the break to the timber and the swamps in the basin—and then they disappeared. Big Ghost was an Indian reservation, without an Indian on it. Fearful spirits, the ghosts of mutilated dead from an ancient battle with Teton Sioux, walked the dark forests of the basin, the Shoshones said. Even broncho Indians stayed clear of Big Ghost.

The cowmen had no rights in the basin; they had been warned repeatedly about trespassing on Indian land, but their cattle were unimpressed by governmental orders. That made the basin a wealthy raiding ground for rustlers from the west prairies, who came through the West Wall in perfectly timed swoops.

For a time the Crowheart ranchers had checked the raids by leaving a man in Big Ghost as look-out. Franks, then Bill Paxton. Baylor knew there was not a man left up here who would volunteer to be the third look-out in Big Ghost—not unless Doc Raven could say what it was a man had to face down there.

They crossed Miller Creek, just west of town. A man on a long-legged blue roan was riding out to meet them. Baylor looked up the street at a small group of men in front of Raven's office, and then across the street at a larger group on the shaded porch of the Shoshone Saloon.

Kullhem spat. "You still say, Baylor, that Baldray ain't behind all this hell?"

"I do." Jim Baldray, the Englishman, owned the I.O.T. His range was fenced all along the break, with permanent camps where the wire winged out. Baldray had the money to keep his wire in place. I.O.T. stuff did not drift down into Big Ghost. There was nothing against the Englishman, Baylor thought, except a sort of jealous resentment that edged toward suspicion.

"You and your brother-in-law don't agree, then," Kullhem said harshly.

Pierce Paxton, the twin brother of the man now lying on Raven's table, was not Baylor's brother-in-law yet, but he would be in another month.

Hap Crosby met them at the lower end of the street. He was the oldest rancher in the country. Sweat was streaking down from his thick, gray sideburns. He looked at Baylor. "Baldray's here. Pierce wants to question him . . . if Raven don't have the answer."

All the Paxtons had been savagely impatient when anger was on them. Pierce, the last one, would ask questions, answer them himself, then go for his pistol. Baldray would be forced to kill him. Pistol work was the first custom of the country the Englishman had learned; and he had mastered it.

"All right, Hap." Baylor looked up the street again. He saw it now. He should have seen it before—the tension there on the Shoshone porch was as tangible as the feel of the hot sun.

"Did Doc . . . has he . . . ?" Orahood asked.

"No, not yet," Crosby said curtly. "Baldray's drinking with that drifter who brought Bill Paxton in."

"Does that mean anything?" Baylor asked evenly.

"I didn't say so, did I?" Crosby answered.

Four other ranchers were waiting with Pierce Paxton at the hitch rail in front of Raven's office. Paxton did not look around. Sharp-featured, tense, his black hat pushed back on thick, brown, curly hair, he kept staring at the doorway of the Shoshone. He was wound up, dangerous. He was fixing to get himself buried with his brother that afternoon, Baylor thought.

Slowly, sullenly, Arn Kullhem said: "By God, I think he's right."

"How far would you go to back that?" Baylor asked. "Across the street?"

Kullhem's deep-set eyes did not waver. "I wonder sometimes just where you stand in this thing, Baylor."

Old Crosby's features turned fighting-bleak and his voice ran hard with authority when he said: "Shut up, the both of you! We got trouble enough."

It was the slamming of Doc Raven's back door, and then the whining of his well sheave that broke the scene and gave both Baylor and Kullhem a chance to look away from each other.

The ranchers stood there in the hot strike of the sun, listening to the doctor washing his hands. Orahood's spittle clung to his lips, and a grayness began to underlay his blisters. A few of the loafers from the Shoshone porch started across the street.

Doc Raven came around the corner of his building, wiping his hands on his shirt. He was a brisk, little, gray-haired man who had come to the country to retire from medicine and study geology.

"Well?" Kullhem rumbled, even before Raven reached the group.

Raven shook his head. His eyes were quick, sharp; his skin thinly laid and pink, as if it never required shaving. "He was smashed by at least a dozen blows, any one of which would have caused death. His clothing was literally knocked from him, not ripped off. I can't even guess what did it."

The sweat on Crosby's cheeks had coursed down through dust and was hanging in little drops on the side of his jaw. "Maybe a grizzly, Doc?"

Raven took a corncob pipe from his pocket. He nodded. "A silver bear would have the power, yes. But there isn't so much as a puncture or a claw mark on Paxton."

"No bear then," Orahood muttered.

Raven scratched a match on the hitch rail. "It's like those other two cases. I don't know what killed any of them."

With one eye on Pierce Paxton, Baylor asked: "Could it be he was thrown from a cliff first, then . . . ?"

"No," Raven said. "Those granite cliffs would have left rock particles ground into the clothes and flesh."

Pierce Paxton had turned his head to watch the doctor. Now he started across the street. Baylor caught his arm and stopped him.

"No, Pierce. You're off on the wrong foot."

Paxton's face was like a wedge. "The hell! How much of *your* stuff was in Baldray's holding corral that time?"

Baylor said: "You know his men had pushed that stuff out of the wire angle. There was a man on his way to Crow Tracks to tell you when you and Bill happened by the I.O.T."

"That's right, Pierce," Crosby said.

"Say it was, then." Paxton's lips were thin against his teeth. "I want to ask Baldray how it happens he can ride into Big Ghost, camp out there whenever he pleases, and ride out again, but Franks and my brother . . . ?"

"I ride it, too," Raven said.

Paxton backed a step away from Baylor. "They know damned well, Doc, that you're just looking for rocks!"

"Who are *they?*" Kullhem asked.

"That's what I'm going to ask Baldray." Paxton knocked Baylor's hand away and started across the street. One of the loafers had already scurried inside. Baylor walked beside Paxton, talking in a low voice. The words did no good, and then Baldray was standing in the doorway, squinting.

The I.O.T. owner was a long, lean man, without much chin. He wore no hat. His squint bunched little ridges of tanned flesh around his eyes and made him appear near-sighted, almost simple. The last two to make an error about that expression had been drifting toughs, who jeered Baldray as a foreigner until they finally got a fight out of him. It had lasted two shots, both Baldray's.

Baldray blinked rapidly. "Not you also, Baylor?"

Paxton stopped, set himself.

The Englishman stayed clear of the doorway.

"Baldray . . . ," Paxton said.

Baylor's rope-scarred right hand hit Paxton under the ear. The blow landed him on his side in the dust. Crosby and Doc Raven came running.

"Give a hand here!" Raven said crisply. Two of them stepped out to help carry Paxton away.

"The hotel," Crosby said. He looked back at Baylor. "I can handle him now."

Baldray smiled uncertainly. "Come have a drink, men!"

Across the street, the little knot of ranchers stared silently. Then Kullhem swung up, and said something to the others in a low voice. Orahood was the last. Baylor went into the Shoshone.

The gloom of the big room reminded him of the silent, waiting forests of Big Ghost. He stood at the bar beside Baldray, who was half a head taller. Kreider, who had found Bill Paxton at the edge of the timber in Battleground Park, took his drink with him toward a table. A man in his middle twenties, Baylor guessed. The rough black beard made him appear older. Just a drifting rider?

Baldray poured the drinks. "Hard business, Baylor, a moment ago. I would have been forced to shoot him."

"Yeah." Baylor took his drink.

"Raven found nothing?"

"Nothing . . . just like the two others. What do you make of it, Baldray?"

The Englishman's horsy face was thoughtful. He smoothed the silky strands of his pale hair. "A beast. It must be an animal of some kind. As a young man in Africa I saw things you would not believe, Baylor, but I still contend there must have been credible explanations. . . . And yet there are strange things that are never explained, and they leave you wondering forever."

There was a hollow chord in Baldray's voice, and it left a chill on Baylor's spine when he thought of Big Ghost and of the way Bill Paxton had been smashed.

"The rustlers always did steal in and out of the basin, of

189

course," Baldray said. "They nearly ruined me before I fenced the break and hired a big crew. You fellows made it nip-and-tuck by keeping a scout down there, but now with this thing getting your men. . . ." Baldray poured another drink.

The "thing" rammed hard at Baylor's mind.

"Isn't it sort of strange that this animal gets just our men, Baldray? After this last deal we won't be able to find a rider with guts enough to stay overnight in the basin. That means we'll be cleaned out properly."

Baldray nodded. "It does appear that this thing is working for the rustlers . . . or being used by them, perhaps. The solution, of course, is to have Big Ghost declared Public Domain."

"Fifty years from now."

"It's possible sooner, perhaps." Baldray's face took on a deeper color. "Fence. I'll lend what's needed for thirty miles. Damn it, Baylor, we're all neighbors!"

He had made the offer before, and Kullhem had growled it down in a ranchers' meeting. Fencing was not all the answer for the little owners. It was all right for I.O.T. because Baldray could afford a big crew, and because the cattle of other ranchers were drifting into the basin. Shut all the drifting over the break-off, and then the rustlers would be cutting wire by night. The smaller ranchers could not hire men enough to stop that practice.

Baylor looked glumly at his glass. The immediate answer to the problem was to go into Big Ghost and find out what was making it impossible to keep a look-out there. He walked across to Kreider.

"Would you ride down with me to where you found Bill Paxton?"

No man could simulate the unease that stirred on

Kreider's dark face. "You figure to come out before dark?"

"Why?"

"You could tell that this Paxton had been in his blankets when he got it. He shot his pistol empty before. . . ." Kreider took his drink quickly. "No, I don't guess I want to go down into the basin, even in daylight . . . not for a while." He looked at Baldray. "You don't run stuff down there, do you, Mister Baldray?"

Baldray shook his head.

So the Englishman had hired this man, Baylor thought. There was nothing unusual about that, but yet it left an uneasy movement in Baylor's mind. "You're afraid to go down there, huh?" he asked.

Kreider stared into space. "Uhn-huh," he said. "Right now I am." He was still looking at something in his own mind when Baylor went out.

II

She was young, with red-gold hair and an eye-catching fullness in the right places. She could ride like a demon, and sometimes she cursed like one. Ken Baylor looked at his sister across the supper table at Hitchrack, and then he slammed his fist hard against the wood.

"Sherry!" he said, "I'll paddle your pants like Pop used to if you ever even think about riding down there again!"

"Can it. Your face might freeze like that."

Baylor leaned back in his chair, glowering. After a few moments, he asked: "Where was this moccasin track?"

"By a rotted log, just south of where Bill Paxton had camped."

No Indian. Raven sometimes wore moccasins.

"There was a mound of earth where Bill's fire had been. Smoothed out."

Kreider had mentioned the mound, but not the smoothness. "At least, that puts a man into it," Baylor said.

Sherry gave him a quick, narrow look. "You felt it?"

"Felt what?"

"A feeling that something is waiting down there, that maybe those Shoshone yarns are not so silly, after all." She hurried on. "Sure, I know whatever it is must be related in some way to the rustling, but just the same. . . ." After a long silence she spoke again. "No one would go with you, huh?"

"Orahood. Just to prove that he wasn't scared."

After he had left Crowheart that morning, Baylor had found the ranchers meeting at Kullhem's. If it had not been for Crosby, they would not have invited him to get down; and even then, desperate, on the edge of ruin, they had been suspicious, both of Baylor and each other.

"Old Hap Crosby wasn't afraid, was he?" Sherry asked.

"No. But he wasn't sure that getting this thing would cure the rustling. He favored more pressure on the territorial representatives to have Big Ghost thrown out as reservation land. Then we could camp down there in force."

The others had ideas of their own, but threaded through all the talk had been the green rot of distrust—and fear of Big Ghost Basin. Baylor told Sherry about it.

"Damned idiots!" she said. "In their hearts they know that Baldray . . . or no other rancher up here . . . is mixed in with the rustlers!"

Baylor hoped it was that way. He got up to help with the dishes, stalling to the last. They heard Gary Owen, one of Hitchrack's three hands, come in from riding the break.

"Take *him*," Sherry said. "He's not afraid of the devil himself."

Baylor nodded.

"I'm going to Crowheart," Sherry said. "If Pierce still wants trouble with Baldray, it will start in town . . . except that I'll see it doesn't start." She rode away a little later, calling back: "So long, Bat-Ears! Be careful down there."

Owen's brown face tightened when he heard the "down there." He was standing at the corral with Baylor. "You headed into the Ghost?" he asked.

"Tonight."

"Saw two men on the Snake Hip Trail today, a long ways off." Owen removed his dun Scottish cap, replaced it. He lit a short-stemmed pipe. "Want me to go along?" He forced it out.

Baylor tried to be casual. "One man will do better, Gary."

"Say so, and I'll go!"

Baylor shook his head. They could not smooth it out with talk.

Three times the ranchers had gone over the escarpment in daylight, ready for full-scale battle. On the second try they had found horse tracks leading away from cattle bunched for a drive through the West Wall. Crosby claimed the rustlers had a man in the basin at all times, watching the break. Baylor thought so, too. But the idea had been lost in the general distrust of each other after the third failure.

Baylor was not thinking of men as the neck of the dun sloped away from him on this night descent in the huge puddle of waiting blackness. The night and Big Ghost were working on him long before he reached the first stream in the basin.

He stopped, listening. The tiny fingers of elementary fear began to test for climbing holds along the crevices of Baylor's brain. He swung in the saddle, and, when he put his pistol away, he told himself that he was a fool.

Shroud moss hanging across the trail touched his face. He tore at it savagely in the instant before he gained control. He came from the trees into the first park. War Dance Creek was running on his right, sullenly, without splash or leap.

All the streams down here were like that. *Imagination,* Baylor argued. He had come over the break unseen. The moss proved he was the first one down the trail in some time. *The first rider, maybe. What is behind me now?* Before he could stop himself, he whirled so quickly he startled the dun.

Back there was blackness, utter quiet. He strained to see, and his imagination prodded him. There was cold sweat on his face. He cursed himself for cowardice.

Where the trail crossed the creek, he would turn into dense timber and stake out for the night. He was here, safe. There was nothing he could do tonight. In the morning. . . .

It was night when the thing got Paxton. . . .

The dun's right forehoof made a sucking sound. The animal stumbled. There was no quick jar of the saddle under Baylor, and he knew, even as he kicked free and jumped, that the stumble had been nothing, that the horse had bent his knee to recover balance before he was clear of leather.

Baylor stood in the wet grass, shaken by the realization of how deeply wound with fear he was. The dun nosed him questioningly. He patted the trim, warm neck and mounted again. If there were anything behind him, the dun would be uneasy.

"There are strange things that will never be explained,

Baylor. . . ."—Baldray had said that in the Shoshone, and now Baylor was sure he had not been mocking him or trying to plant an idea.

Baylor spent the night sitting against a tree, with his blankets draped around him. The dun was tied on the other side of the tree. Baylor's carbine was close at hand, lying on the sheepskin of the saddle skirts. The carbine was too small of caliber, Baylor thought, too small for what he was looking for. What *was* he looking for? Out of the dead silence, from the ancient, waiting forest, came another chilling question. *What is looking for you, Baylor?*

The night walked slowly, on cold feet. It passed at last. Baylor rose stiffly. He ate roast beef from his sack and finished with a cold boiled potato. Raven was the only other man he knew who liked a cold spud. Raven had come to the Crowheart country just about the time cattle rustling began in earnest, after a long period of inactivity.

The nameless fears that had passed were now replaced with the suspicions of the conscious mind.

Early sunlight was killing dew when Baylor rode into Battleground Park. He picked up the tracks of Sherry's little mare, coming into the park from the Snake Hip Trail. Owen had seen two riders on the Snake Hip the day before, but there was no sign that they come this far. He followed Sherry's trail straight to where Paxton had been killed.

Baylor studied the earth mound over the fire site. It was too smooth, and so was the torn ground around it, and, yet, the earth scars still spoke of power and fury and compulsion. An ant hill made a bare spot in the grass not fifteen feet away. Paxton would have used that. Because of the nature of his business here he would have had it figured in advance.

Baylor picked up a tip cluster of pine needles. He stared at the spruces. Their lower branches were withered, but here was broken freshness from high above. He went slowly among the trees close to the fire site. Here and there Paxton had broken dead limbs for his fire, but there was no evidence that anything had come down from the high branches.

He tossed the tip cluster away and went south of the camp to the rich, brown mark of a rotted log. There were Sherry's tracks again, but no moccasin print.

Out in the grass the dun whirled uptrail. Baylor drew his pistol and stepped behind a tree. A little later Baldray, wearing a fringed buckskin shirt, rode into the park with Doc Raven.

"We knew your horse," Raven said. He was wearing Shoshone moccasins, Baylor observed.

Baldray's face turned bone-bleak when he saw a jumper fragment on a bush. "Oh! This is the place, eh?" He swung down easily. "Let's have a look, Raven."

The doctor moved briskly. "The devil!" he muttered. "See how the fire has been covered." His smooth, pink face was puzzled. He picked up the piece of jumper. "Good Lord!"

Baldray's heel struck the tip cluster of pine needles and punched them into the soft earth. "Did you discover anything, Baylor?"

"Nothing." Baylor shook his head. Raven's saddlebags appeared to be already filled with rocks. Gary Owen said the doctor started at the escarpment and tried to haul half the country with him every time he went out. "You fellows came down the Snake Hip?"

Raven was studying tree burls. "We started in yesterday," he said, "but I had forgotten a manual I needed, so we rode out last evening." He looked at Baldray. "You know, James, in the big burn along the cliffs I've seen jack-pine seeds completely embedded in the trunks. I have a theory. . . ."

"Rocks, this time," Baldray said. "If you want to look at that quartz on the West Wall before night, you'd better forget the tree seeds." He blinked. "Tree seeds? Now isn't that odd?"

When the two men rode west, Baylor stared at their backs, not knowing just what he thought.

III

Baylor spent the day working the edges of the swamps along lower War Dance. Cattle were wallowing everywhere. He was nagged by not knowing what he was looking for; he had expected to find some sign where Paxton had been killed, at least the moccasin track.

At sunset he came out in the big burn. Several years before, Indians had thrown firebrands from the cliffs to start a fire to drive game from the basin. The wind had veered, and the fire, instead of crowning across the basin, had roared along the cliffs in a mile-wide swath. That cured the Indians. Evil spirits, they said, had blown a mighty breath to change the wind.

With the bare cliffs at his back, Baylor looked across the spear points of the trees. The parks were green islands, the largest being Battleground Park, where Paxton had died. The West Wall was far to his right, a red granite barrier that appeared impassable, but there were breaks in it, he knew, the holes where Crowheart cattle seeped away.

About a half mile air-line a gray horse came to the edge

of one of the emerald parks. Bill Paxton had ridden a gray into Big Ghost. Kreider had brought out only the rig.

Once down in the timber, it took an hour of steady searching before Baylor found the right park. The limping gray knee-high in grass was Paxton's horse, all right. It saw Baylor when he led the dun from the timber. It snorted and broke like a wild animal for cover. There was never a chance to catch it.

Baylor recoiled his rope, listening to the gray crashing away like a frightened elk. The horse had not been here long enough to go mustang. The terror of the night thing had got Bill Paxton was riding on the gray.

Night was coming now. Gloom was crouched among the trees. The little golden sounds of day were dead. You are afraid, Big Ghost said. You will be like Paxton's horse if you stay here.

Baylor went through a neck of timber between parks. In the dying light on lower War Dance he cut his own trail of the morning. Beside the dun's tracks, in the middle of a mud bar, he saw a round imprint. He hung low in the saddle to look. A man wearing moccasins had been on his trail. Here man had leaped halfway across the mud bar, putting down only the toes and the ball of one foot to gain purchase for another jump to where the grass left no mark. The foot had slid a trifle forward when it struck, and so there was no way to estimate how large—or small—it had been.

Baylor was relieved. He could deal with a man, even one who used Indian tricks like that. If this fellow wanted to play hide-and-seek, Baylor would take him on—and catch him in the end, and find out why the man had erased the track that Sherry had seen.

Dog-tired, he made a cold camp far enough from War

Dance so that the muttering water would not cover close sounds. He freed the dun to graze, ate a cold meal, and rolled up in his blankets. A wind ran through the timber.

Baylor rolled a smoke, and then he crumpled it. The scent of tobacco smoke would drift a long way to guide a man creeping in.

No man killed Paxton or the others.

Baylor lay wide awake, straining at the darkness, for a long time, until finally he slept from sheer exhaustion.

The morning sun was a wondrous friend. Baylor slopped the icy water of the stream against his face. The dun came from the wet grass and greeted him.

He rode south, then swung toward the West Wall, crossing parks he had never seen before. He took it slowly, not watching his back trail. In the middle of the day, after crossing a park just like a dozen others, he dismounted in the timber and crept back to make a test.

For an hour he waited behind a windfall. The first sound came, the breaking of a stick on the other side of the tiny green spot. Baylor had been half dozing by then. *Too easy,* he thought, *something is wrong.* He heard hoofs on the needle mat.

He had expected a man on foot. He crawled away and ran back to the dun, placing one hand on its nose, ready for the gentle pressure that would prevent a whinny. A little later he heard sounds off to his left. The man was going around, sticking to the timber. Slowly Baylor led his horse to intercept the sounds. The other man came slowly, also, and then Baylor caught the movement of a sorrel, saw an outline of its rider.

He dropped the reins then and went in as quickly as he could. He made noise. The dun whinnied. The other rider hit the ground. A carbine blasted, funneling pulp from a tree ahead of Baylor. He shot toward the sound with his pistol. The sorrel reared, then bolted straight ahead.

It flashed across a relatively open spot. It was Pierce Paxton's stallion. "Oh, God!" Baylor muttered: "Pierce." Then he yelled: "Pierce!"

There was silence before the answer came. "Baylor?" It was Pierce Paxton. He was unshaven, red-eyed. He said: "Who the hell did you think you were trying to take?"

Baylor put his pistol away. "Moccasin Joe. Who were you shooting at?"

"Anybody that tried to close in on me like that!" Tenseness was still laid flat on Paxton's thin features. "Who's Moccasin Joe?"

Baylor told everything he knew about the man.

Paxton shook his head, staring around him at the trees. "It's not Raven. I've been watching him and Baldray from the time they went across Agate Park."

"Why?"

Paxton stared. "You know why." He rubbed his hand across his eyes. "I think maybe I was wrong. We lost two men down here, Baylor, but Baldray and Raven never had any trouble. Now I know why. They got a cabin hidden in the rocks near the West Wall. They don't stay out in the open." Paxton saw the quick suspicion on Baylor's face.

"Uhn-huh, I thought so, too, at first, Ken. I thought they knew what's loose down here . . . that they were hooked up with the rustlers. I watched them for a day and a half. All they did was pound quartz rock and laugh like two kids. They may be crazy, Baylor, but I don't think they're hooked up with the rustlers."

Paxton rubbed his eyes again. "Made a fool of myself the other day, didn't I? What did Sherry say?"

"Nothing much. We both made fools of ourselves a minute ago, Pierce. . . . Let's catch your horse."

The stallion had stopped in the next park west. Paxton went in and towed the horse back on the run. It saw the dun and tried to break over to start trouble. Paxton sawed down brutally on the bit before he got the horse quieted. That was not like Paxton. The nights down here had worked on his nerves, too.

They went back to the timber and sprawled out. Paxton lay with his hands over his face.

"How you fixed for grub?" Baylor asked.

"Ran out yesterday." Paxton heard Baylor rustling in his gunny sack. "I'm not hungry." But he finally ate, and he kept looking sidewise at Baylor until he asked: "You've been here two nights?"

"Yeah."

"Any trouble?"

"Scared myself some," Baylor said. "Did you?"

"I didn't have to. Since the first night I spent here, I've been jumping three feet every time a squirrel cut loose. I had a little fire on Hellion Creek that night, with a couple of hatfuls of wet sand, just in case."

Paxton had started with a defensive edge to his voice, but now it was gone and his bloodshot eyes were tight. "The stallion just naturally raised hell. He got snarled up on his picket rope and almost paunched himself on a snag. I got him out of that, and then I doused the fire.

"From the way the horse moved and pointed, I knew something was prowling. It went all around the camp, and once I heard it brush a tree."

The hackles on Baylor's neck were up.

"You know how a lion will do that," Paxton said. He shook his head. "No lion. The next morning, in some fresh dirt where a squirrel had been digging under a tree, I saw a track"—Paxton put his hands side by side—"like that, Ken. No pads . . . just a big mess!" Paxton's hands were shaking. "What was it, Baylor? The thing that got Bill?"

The thing. What else could a man call it? Baylor thought. He said: "There's an explanation to everything."

"Explain it, then!"

"Take it easy, Pierce. We'll get it."

The thought of action always helped steady Paxton. "How?" he asked.

"First, we'll get this Moccasin Joe." Baylor thought of something so clear he wondered how he had missed it. "Did you stop in Battleground Park?"

"I didn't come down the Snake Hip."

"Old Moccasin Joe has trailed me once, and now I think I know why." The thought carried a little chill. "Here's what we'll do, Paxton. . . ."

Later, Baylor divided the food. It would be parched corn, now, and jerky, about enough for two days, if a man did not care how hungry he got. "Day after tomorrow," Baylor said.

They rode away in different directions, Baylor going back to Battleground Park. He found the tip-cluster that Baldray had stepped on, and dug it out of the earth and held it only a moment before dropping it again. Pine needles. Everything here was spruce. The fact had not registered the first time.

That tip cluster had come from a branch that Moccasin Joe had used to brush out sign. Probably he had carried the branch from across the creek. Moccasin Joe knew what the thing was. He was covering up for it.

The dun whinnied. Baldray was riding into the lower end of the park. He veered over when he saw Baylor's horse.

"You haven't moved!" Baldray grinned to show he was joking. He was clean-shaven. He appeared rested, calm.

That came easier when a man slept in a cabin and ate his fill, Baylor thought.

"You look done in," Baldray said.

"I'm all right."

Baldray squinted at the fringes of his beaded shirt. His face began to redden. "It's no good sleeping out. Bumps and things, you know. I have a cabin near the West Wall. Built it four years ago. Raven's there now. I wish you'd use it, Baylor. I'll tell you how to find it."

Paxton had taken care of that. "I know," Baylor said.

Baldray blinked. "Oh!" He raised pale brows. "Well, yes. I've been a little selfish. Reservation land, so-called. If the fact got around that someone had built here. . . ."

Baylor picked up the tip cluster. "What kind of a tree is that from?"

Baldray squinted. "Evergreen."

"Spruce or pine?"

The Englishman laughed. "You and Raven! I know evergreen from canoe birch, but that's about all."

Baldray was one Englishman who had not run for home after the big die-ups of the no-Chinook years. He should know pine needles from spruce, but maybe he did not.

Baldray's face was stone-serious when he asked: "Any luck?"

Baylor shook his head.

"There are harsh thoughts about me." Baldray's voice was crisp. "Fifteen years here and I'm still not quite a resident, except with you and Crosby." Baldray looked around the park. "This won't be reservation always. Room for

I.O.T. down here, as well as the rest . . . once the rustlers are dealt with, and the government sees the light." Baldray slouched in the saddle, rolling a cigarette. "I have watched the breaks in the West Wall from the rocks near my cabin. There is a sort of pattern to the way the scoundrels come and go. I would say, Baylor . . . it is a guess, but I would say . . . the next raid might be due to go out through Windy Trail." His smoke rolled and lit, Baldray started away. "Windy Trail. I'm going to tell Crosby, some of the others. Good name, Crosby. English, you know."

He rode away.

IV

It was not entirely hunger that made Baylor's stomach tighten as he rode across the burn the next afternoon. Like the others, the night before had been a bad one, with his mind and the deep, still forests speaking to him. He did not know now whether or not he was being trailed, but he had played the game all the way, and, if Paxton had done his part, things might come off as planned.

Paxton was there, crouched in the rocks near the east side of the burn. They exchanged clothes behind the jumble of fire-chipped stone.

"I went out," Paxton said. "Sherry wants to see you to-morrow morning in Battleground Park."

"Why didn't you talk her out of it?"

"You know better." Paxton was stuffing newspaper under the sweatband of Baylor's hat.

"What does she want?"

"I don't know. She told me to go to hell when I ordered her not to come down here. Then she rode over to I.O.T. to see Baldray. I left a note in the bunkhouse for Gary Owen to come here with her."

They were dressed.

"Keep in plain sight on the burn," Baylor said. "And keep going."

"All right." Paxton took the reins. "Kullhem found out that Kreider was riding with the rustlers on the west prairie two weeks ago."

"Fine. Just right. Get going."

He watched Paxton ride away, past the black snags and leaning trees. The dun had gone into the rocks and the dun had gone out a few minutes later, and the rider was dressed exactly as he had been when going in. It might work, if Moccasin Joe was still trailing with his little pine-branch broom. The dirty bastard.

The sun died behind the red West Wall. A wind came down across the rocks and stirred the tiny jack-pines in the burn. Murk crept into basin.

The man came from sparse timber at the east edge of the burn. Buckskins. Probably moccasins. Long yellow hair under a slouch hat. He paused and looked up where the dun had disappeared two hours before.

Baylor watched from a crack between the rocks. The man came clear, lifting his body easily over fallen trees. He walked straight at the rocks, then swung a little to the uphill side. Baylor drew his pistol and took a position behind a rock where the man would likely pass.

The steps were close, just around the rock. They stopped. With his stomach sucked in, breathing through a wide-open mouth, Baylor waited to fit the next soft scrape to the man's position. Silence pinched at nerve ends before the fellow moved again.

In two driving steps Baylor went around the rock. He

was just a fraction late, almost on top of a beard-matted face, two startled eyes and that tangle of yellow hair. He swung the pistol.

Moccasin Joe went back like a cat, clutching a knife in his belt. Baylor's blow missed. The pistol rang on rock, and by then the knife was coming clear. Baylor drove in with his shoulder turned. The knife was coming down when the shoulder caught the man at the throat lacing of his shirt.

Baylor was on top when they went down. He got the knife arm then, and suddenly threw all his power into a side push. The man's hand went against the rock. Baylor began to grind it along the granite. The rock was running red before Moccasin Joe dropped the knife. With the explosive strength of a deer, he arched his body, throwing Baylor sidewise against the rock. One of the man's knees doubled back like a trap spring, then the foot lashed out and knocked Baylor away.

Moccasin Joe leaped up. He did not run. He dived in. Baylor caught him with a heeled hand under the chin. The man's head snapped back, but his weight came on. A knee struck Baylor in the groin. Sick with the searing agony of it, Baylor grabbed the long hair with both hands. He kept swinging Moccasin Joe's head into the rock until there was no resistance but limp weight.

For several moments Baylor lay under the weight, grinding his teeth in pain, and then he pushed free, straightening up by degrees, stabbing his feet against the ground. The front sight of his pistol was smeared, the muzzle burred, and maybe the barrel was bent a little.

But he had the man who was going to tell him what was killing ranch scouts in Big Ghost Basin. Except for the knife, Moccasin Joe had carried no other weapon. Baylor cut the fellow's belt and tied his hands behind him. Blood was smeared in the tangled yellow hair.

Baylor had never seen him before.

Going down the burn, the prisoner was wobbly, but he was walking steadily enough before they reached the park, where Paxton was to come soon after dark. It was almost dark now. Just inside the timber, Baylor made Joe lie down, then tied his ankles with Paxton's belt.

Firelight was a blessed relief after black, cold nights. "The first man killed here was one of yours, Joe," Baylor said. "You boys got on to something that makes it impossible for us to keep a man here. What is it?"

After a long silence Baylor removed one of his prisoner's moccasins. The man's eyes rolled as he stared at the fire. Baylor squatted by the flames, turning the knife slowly in the heat until the thin edge of the blade was showing dull red.

Where the hell was Pierce Paxton?

"Put out the fire," Moccasin Joe said.

"Talk some more." Baylor kept turning the blade. "That first man was one of yours, wasn't he?"

"Yeah." Moccasin Joe was beginning to sweat. The skin above his beard was turning dirty yellow.

Baylor lifted the knife to let him see it. "Your thing has got us stopped," Baylor said. "What is it?"

The firelight ran on a growing fear in the captive's eyes. He started to speak, and then he lay back.

"First, the flat of the blade against the bottom of your arch, then the point between the hock and the tendon. I'll reheat each time, of course." Even to Baylor his own words seemed to carry conviction.

"Put the fire out!"

Baylor lifted the knife again. The blade was bright red. "I saw Teton Sioux do this once," he lied calmly.

Moccasin Joe's breath was coming hard.

"You covered up something where Paxton was killed, didn't you? And then you checked back and wiped out a track of your own that you had overlooked."

"Yeah."

"Keep talking."

"I want a smoke. I won't tell you anything until I get a smoke!"

Baylor stared at the tangled face, at the terror in the man's eyes. For a customer as tough as this one had proved up in the rocks, he was softening pretty fast under a torture bluff.

Baylor laid the knife where the blade would stay hot. He rolled two smokes and lit them. He put one in Moccasin Joe's mouth.

"You got to untie my hands."

"You can smoke without that."

The cigarette stuck to the captive's lips. He tried to roll it free and it fell into his beard. He jerked his head back and the smoke fell to the ground. Baylor put it back in the man's mouth. He untied the fellow's hands.

Moccasin Joe sat up and puffed his cigarette, rolling his shoulders.

"Let's have it," Baylor said.

"The bunch that's been raiding here ain't the one from the west prairie, like you think. We been hanging out on the regular reservation. The agent is getting his cut."

It sounded like a quickly made-up lie. "Is Kreider one of the bunch?"

The captive hesitated. "Sure."

"Describe him."

Moccasin Joe did that well enough.

"What killed Paxton?"

"Which one was he?"

"The last one . . . in Battleground Park."

"I'll tell you." Moccasin Joe made sucking sounds, trying to get smoke from a dead cigarette.

Baylor took a twig from the fire. He leaned down. The captive's hands came up from his lap like springs. They clamped behind Baylor's neck and jerked. At the same time Moccasin Joe ducked his own head. Baylor came within an ace of getting his face smashed against hard bone. He spread his hands between his face and the battering block just in time. Even so, he felt his nose crunch, and it seemed that every tooth in his mouth was loosened. He was in a crouch then, and Moccasin Joe's thumbs were digging at his throat. Baylor drove his right knee straight ahead.

Moccasin Joe's hands loosened. He fell back without a sound. Baylor stood there rubbing his knee. He could not stand on the leg for a while. The sensitive ligaments above the cap had struck squarely on the point of Moccasin Joe's jaw.

Once more Baylor cinched the man's arms tightly behind his back. Let him die for want of a smoke. Blood dripped into the fire as Baylor put on more wood. He stared at the red-hot knife, wishing for just an instant that he was callous enough to use it.

Where in hell is Paxton? he thought.

Blood began to stream down his lips. He felt his way to the creek and washed his face and dipped cold water down the back of his neck. After a while the bleeding stopped. Both sides of his nose were swollen so that he could not breathe through them. His lips were cut. *I'm lucky,* he told himself, *getting out with only a busted nose after falling for an old gag like that. You're not out of it yet, Baylor. It's night again.*

Once more the old voices of Big Ghost were running in his mind. Baylor dipped Paxton's hat full of water and went back to the fire and Moccasin Joe.

"Sit up if you want a drink."

It was a struggle for Moccasin Joe, but he made it. His eyes were still a little hazy, but clear enough to look at Baylor with hatred.

Baylor took the knife from the fire and stood over his captive, tapping his boot against the man's bare foot. Moccasin Joe looked at the glowing steel, and then at Baylor. His eyes showed no fear.

"You ain't got the guts."

The bluff was no good. Baylor threw the knife into the ground near the fire. "I've got guts enough to help hang you," he said. "We know you're one of the rustlers, and we know you've been doing chores for the thing in the basin that's killed our men. Better loosen up, Joe."

"My name ain't Joe."

"That won't make any difference when you swing."

"Talk away, cowboy."

He's not afraid of me, Baylor thought, *but it's up in his neck because of what he knows is out there.* It's out there, the night said.

Paxton should be coming. He should have been here an hour ago.

He went to the edge of the park, listening for the hoof sounds of the dun. There was nothing in the park but ancient night and aching quiet. Grunting sounds and the creaking of twigs sent Baylor running back to the fire. Moccasin Joe was trying to get away, pushing himself by digging his heels into the ground. He had gone almost twenty feet.

Baylor hauled him back to the fire. The man's muscles were jerking. "They'll kill me," he said, "but that'll be the best way. Put out the fire. I'll tell you!"

"You've pulled a couple of fast ones already."

"Put it out!"

Brutal fear came like a bad odor from the man. Baylor's back was crawling. He turned toward the creek to get another hatful of water.

Twigs popped. Something *thudded* softly out in the forest.

"It's coming! Turn me loose!" Moccasin Joe's voice rose in a hoarse, quavering scream. "O Jesus . . . !" And then he was silent.

V

Standing at the edge of firelight, with his bent-barreled pistol in his hand, Baylor was in a cold sweat.

Paxton's voice came from the forest. "Baylor!"

"Here!" Baylor made two efforts before he got the pistol back in leather. By the time Paxton came in, leading the dun, Baylor's fear had turned to anger.

"Did you make another trip out to visit and have a shave!"

Paxton was in no light mood, either. His face was swelling from mosquito bites. He had clawed at them and smeared mud from his hairline to his throat. "I got bogged down in a stinking swamp! Lost your carbine there, too." He looked at Moccasin Joe. "I see you got. . . . What ails him?"

Moccasin Joe's eyes were set, unseeing. His jaw was jerking and little strings of saliva were spilling into his beard.

Mice feet tracked on Baylor's spine. "Ummm!" he said

in a long breath. "He thought you were the thing!"

"The thing! Good God!" Paxton's eyes rolled white in his mud-smeared face. His voice dropped. "Your horse raised hell back there a minute ago."

The dun was shuddering now, its ears set toward the creek. It was ready to bolt. Paxton drew his pistol.

"Put that popgun away!" Baylor cried. "Help me get him on the horse!" He grabbed the knife and slashed the belt around Joe's ankles. "Stand up!"

The man rose obediently, numbly, his jaw still working. Paxton leaped to grab the dun's reins when the horse tried to bolt toward the park.

Baylor threw Moccasin Joe across the saddle of the plunging horse.

"Lead the horse out of here!"

They crashed toward the park, with the horse fighting to get away, with Baylor fighting to keep Moccasin Joe across the saddle. The dun tried to bolt until they were in timber at the lower end of the park, and then it quieted.

"How far to the cabin where Raven is?" Baylor asked.

"Maybe four miles," Paxton answered. "I won't try no short cuts through a swamp this time." He laughed shakily.

They spoke but little as they moved through the deep night of Big Ghost Basin. Baylor walked behind now. Paxton broke off a limb and used it as a feeler overhead when they were in timber. Each time he said—"Limb!"— they heard Moccasin Joe grunt a little as he ducked against the horn.

Baylor guessed it was well after midnight when Paxton stopped in the rocks and said: "It's close to here . . . some place. I'll go ahead and see."

Baylor was alone. He heard Paxton's footsteps fade into the rocks. The dun was droop-headed now. Moccasin Joe was a dark lump in the saddle.

Relief ran through Baylor when he heard the mumble of voices somewhere ahead, and presently Paxton came back. "The cabin is about a hundred yards from here. Raven's there."

Paxton took care of the dun. Raven and Baylor led the captive inside. Moccasin Joe was like a robot. Light from a brass Rivers lamp showed a four-bunk lay-out, with a large fireplace at one end. There was a shelf of books near the fireplace, and rock specimens scattered everywhere else.

Raven's hair was rumpled. He was in his undershirt and boots. His pink face was shining and his eyes were sharp. He looked at Moccasin Joe and said: "I thought *I* brought in specimens."

Moccasin Joe was staring.

Raven took the man's right hand and looked at the grated knuckles. He stood on tiptoe to peer at the marks where Baylor had banged Moccasin Joe's head against the rock.

"I roughed him up," Baylor said.

"You didn't hurt him." Raven passed his hand before the man's face. "Oregon! Oregon!" he said.

"Huh?" the man said dully.

"You know him?" Baylor asked.

"I saw him out on the west prairie a month ago, camped with a group of men. They called him that."

"Rustlers, eh?"

"Probably. I ride where I like. Nobody bothers me. I've doctored a man or two out that way, without asking his business."

"What's wrong with this one?" Baylor asked.

"Shock. His mind, roughly, is locked on something. Did you try to scare him to death?"

"Not me. Something scared the hell out of me, and Paxton, too. Maybe if we'd known what it was, we'd be like Mocc . . . Oregon."

Paxton came in. Raven glanced at his face. "Wash it off and quit scratching the lumps, Paxton. Get some grease out of the jar there by the books." Raven motioned Oregon toward a chair. "Sit down there."

Doc Raven went to work. He cleansed and dressed Oregon's hand, and took care of the cuts on his head, shearing into the long hair with evident satisfaction. "Retire," he muttered. "I've got so I don't go to an outbuilding without taking a medical kit along."

Raven was completely happy, Baylor thought.

"Help yourselves to the grub, boys," the doctor said.

Oregon ate mechanically, staring at Raven most of the time. When Raven was briskly directing him into a bunk afterward, the doctor asked casually: "Did Martin get over that dislocated shoulder all right?"

"Yeah," Oregon said, "yeah, he's all right." Then his eyes slipped back to dullness once more.

Raven looked at Paxton and Baylor. "I think he'll be coming out of it after a night's rest. Go to bed. I'll just sit here and read."

"I don't want that man to get away," Baylor said. "He's going to tell me something in the morning."

Raven shook his head. "You won't get anything out of this one, Baylor. I probed two bullets out of his chest once, and he never made a peep." Raven smiled at the suspicious stares of the two ranchers. "I'm a doctor," he said. "Retired." He laughed. "Now go to bed, both of you."

Raven was cooking when Baylor woke up. Paxton was still sound asleep. Oregon was lying in his bunk awake.

There was complete awareness in his eyes when he looked at Baylor.

"Ready to talk?" Baylor asked.

"To hell with you," Oregon said.

Paxton woke up while Baylor was dressing. He took his pistol from under his blankets and walked across the room to Oregon. "That was my brother that was killed by your pet a few days ago."

"Too bad," Oregon said.

Paxton turned toward Baylor. "Let's stake this bastard out by a fire tonight . . . and leave him!"

"That's enough!" Raven's voice cut sharply. "Oregon is yours, but let's have no more of that kind of talk."

"What'll we do?" Paxton asked. "I want to go with you to meet Sherry this morning, and. . . ." He glanced at Raven.

"You stay here," Baylor said. "I'll see Sherry. What the hell does she want?"

The first hot meal in several days was like water in a desert. After breakfast Baylor brought the dun from a barred enclosure where a spring made a green spot in the rocks.

Paxton grumped about being left to watch the prisoner. Sherry would take some of that out of him soon enough, after they were married, Baylor thought.

Baylor went inside for one last word with Oregon. "I know you lied about your bunch hanging out on the reservation, Oregon. How about Kreider?"

"You find out," Oregon said.

Baylor looked at Paxton.

"Don't fret," Paxton said. "I'll watch him, all right."

Raven walked outside with him. "I know how you boys feel, Baylor. Out here you try to make things all black or all white. There's shades between the two, Baylor. I don't defend Oregon. I don't condemn him. You understand?"

"I'm trying to."

"That helps. You want my rifle?"

"Carbine." Baylor shook his head. "Thanks, no."

VI

Sherry and Gary Owen were waiting in Battleground Park when he reached there. It was close to where Bill Paxton had been killed.

"What happened to your nose?" Sherry asked.

"Froze it in the creek. Nice place you picked to meet me."

"Yeah." Owen looked toward the little mound that covered the fire site. "She picked it."

Sherry said: "Did you see anyone last night?"

"Pierce and me met a man, not socially, though. Who do you mean?"

"Any of the ranchers, tight-mouth. They came in last night, the crews from every outfit. Crosby and Baldray got them together. They're going to filter around and trap the rustlers tomorrow or the next day near the West Wall."

"Baldray's idea?" Baylor asked.

Owen nodded. "Him and Kreider."

"Kreider!"

"He's a special agent of the Indian Department," Owen said. "He was sent here to investigate a rumor that the rustlers were operating from reservation land. For a while he was in solid with them. From what we gathered, he's got a chum still with the bunch on the west prairie, and that fellow tipped Kreider off about the next raid."

The rustlers must have caught on to Kreider, Baylor thought. *That was why Oregon had been so willing to identify him as one of the gang. Tomorrow or the next day.* . . . Plenty of time for what Baylor had to do. He looked at a .45-50 Winchester in Owen's saddle boot.

"I'd like to borrow your rifle, Gary."

"I brought one for you," Sherry said. She walked into the grass, and returned with a double-barreled weapon.

Baylor hefted the piece. "One of Baldray's."

"Elephant gun," Sherry said. "A Five Seventy-Seven, whatever that is." She gave her brother, one by one, a half dozen cartridges. "Pierce told me he saw the track of something there that scared him. Where is Pierce?"

His sister was quite a woman, Baylor thought. He told her and Owen about capturing Oregon. "I figure it will be easier to get a line on this thing, now that Oregon is out of the way."

Owen stared at the timber edges of the park. "Thing," he muttered. "I'll stay with you, Ken."

"Take Sherry back to the benches. . . ."

"I know the way," Sherry said. "You know something? Kreider says there's a bill going into the next Congress to make Big Ghost public land again."

"Owen's taking you back to the benches," Baylor said.

"You know who got action started on that bill?" Sherry asked. "Jim Baldray."

"Yeah," Owen said. "Even Kullhem admits now that he must have had the wrong idea about Baldray. I'll stay down here with you, Ken."

"The two of you work well together," Baylor said, "changing the subject, throwing me off. All right, get out of here, Sherry, and be sure you're good and out before night."

The girl got on her horse. Her face was pale under its tan. "Don't depend entirely on that elephant gun, Ken. Get up in a tree, or something."

"I figured on that," Baylor said. "So long, Red."

The two men walked until she disappeared into the timber at the upper end of Battleground Park.

"Fighting rustlers don't scare me no more than a man's got a right to be scared," Owen said abruptly. He dug out his short-stemmed pipe and lit it. "But after I saw Paxton . . . and them other two, I'll admit I didn't have the guts to come down here at night. Now I'm here, I'll stay."

Baylor was glad to have him—with that big-bored Winchester.

"I don't know what we're after," Baylor said. "But maybe in a couple of hours we'll know. Come on."

They went back in the timber, and stayed out of sight until they came to the park below the burn, the place where Baylor had built his fire the night before. The memory of the night began to work on Baylor.

He felt a chill when he saw that the fire he and Paxton had left burning in their quick retreat had been covered with a great heap of dirt and needles. There were long marks in the torn ground, but no sharp imprints. The story was there. The fire had kept on smoldering under the first weight of dirt and dry forest mat, and the thing had continued to throw dirt in a savage frenzy until the smoke had ceased. Fire. That was the magnet.

Owen sucked nervously on his pipe, staring. "What done it?"

Baylor shook his head. "Let's try the soft ground by the creek." They stood on the east bank. Baylor stared at the choke of willows and trees on the other side. Last night he had dipped water from this very spot, and over there, somewhere, the thing had been pacing, circling, working up to coming in. It must have been quite close when he threw Oregon at the dun and ran in terror.

Night will come again, a voice said.

Baylor and Owen stayed close together while they searched. Farther up the stream they found where the thing had leaped the creek in one bound. Four imprints in the muddy bank.

"I'll be dipped in what!" There was a little fracture in Owen's voice. "That ain't no track of nothing I ever seen!"

The outlines were mushy. The mud was firm, but still there was no clear definition of form. The whole thing was a patchwork of bumps and ridges that would not fit any living creature Baylor had ever seen or heard of. "That's no bear," he said.

"Back in Ireland my grandmother used to scare us. . . ." Owen shook his head.

On a limb snag across the creek they found a small patch of short, brittle hair with a scab scale clinging to it.

"There ain't anything in the world with hair like that!" Owen cried.

Here with the shroud moss motionless on gray limbs, in the ancient stillness of Big Ghost, Baylor was again prey to fear of the Unknown, and for a moment there was no civilization because nothing fitted previous experience.

"The rustlers have seen it," he said. "Oregon said it got one of their men. They wouldn't have covered up for it if they hadn't been afraid we might recognize the sign." He stared at Owen. "Fire, Gary. Fire is what brings it."

"I been here at night . . . with fire." Owen hunched his shoulders.

"It's a big hole. A man might be lucky here for a long

time, and then one night. . . . Where are the ranchers going to meet?"

"They'll camp out in little bunches on those timbered hogbacks that point toward the West Wall. When they see Crosby's smoke signal from the Wall. . . ."

"We've got to warn them, Gary. Orahood never spent a night out in his life without building a fire. Get down there and pass the word . . . no fires!"

"That leaves you alone."

"I've been several nights alone. Take the dun with you. I don't want him hurt."

"Holy God, Ken! You don't want the dun hurt, but you. . . ."

"Stick to the timber, Gary, so you won't mess up their trap."

Baylor took both ropes from the saddles. Ready to leave, Owen said: "Take my rifle. That elephant business only shoots twice."

"I'll do better than that, from where I'll be. Tonight you'll like the feel of that big barrel across your knees, Gary."

"Don't scare me. I already know I'm a damned coward. I *want* to leave here, I'll admit it." Owen rode away.

Baylor did not like to admit how alone he felt.

Big Ghost nights always seemed to settle as if they had special purpose in making the basin a black hole. From his platform of laced rope between two limbs of a spruce tree, Baylor peered down to where his pile of wood was ready for a match. He had pulled in other fuel close to the site, enough to keep a fairly large fire all night.

It was about time to light it. The sooner the better. The smoke would make a long trail through the forest, the fumes a little bright spot in the murk, and this thing that must kill fire might be attracted. It would be a cinch from here.

A cinch? Maybe the thing climbs trees.

Baylor climbed down and lit the fire. He waited just long enough to know that it would burn, and then he climbed again to his rope perch. The blackness laughed at his haste. Smoke came up between the ropes and began to choke him. That was a point he had not thought of at all, but presently the fire took hold in earnest, light reached out to touch the gray holes of waiting trees, and a small wind began to drift the smoke at a lower level.

Baylor tried to settle comfortably against the ropes. The sling of the heavy double-barrel was over a limb above him, so the weapon could not fall. The four spare cartridges were buttoned in the breast pocket of his jumper. He felt the cold, big roundness of them when he took out the makings of a cigarette.

It was as dark as a pocket up in the tree. For a while the oddness of being where he was intrigued Baylor, and then he thought of a dozen flaws in his plan. But if it did not work out tonight, he would stay with it until it did. He reached over to touch the .577. The four spare cartridges did not count. He had two shots coming. They should be enough.

Bill Paxton's .45 was empty when Kreider found him.

The night lagged. Big Ghost gathered all its secrets to it, and the darkness whispered. Three times Baylor went down to put wood on the fire. Each time he took the heavy rifle, and each time his flesh crawled until he was back on the rope net once more.

He smoked all his tobacco. Thirst started. He listened to the creek. It was not very far. *Go get yourself a drink, Baylor.* He tried not to listen. His thirst grew out of all proportion, and he knew it was not real. He could not be thirsty; he had drunk enough just before dark.

Get yourself a drink. Don't be a fool.

He waited till the fire needed wood. After building it up, he stood a moment by the tree, with one hand on the rope that led to safety.

Go on, Baylor. Are you afraid to get a drink?

The water was icy cold against the sweat on his face. He drank from cupped hands, then wiped them on his jumper, staring at the blackness across the creek. Last night the thing had been somewhere out there. It might be there now. He took two steps toward the fire. Something splashed in the water behind him. He was cocking the gun and swinging around all the time he knew the splash had come from a muskrat.

For a few moments he stood drying his hands over the heat, a little gesture of striking back at the Unknown. But when he started up the tree, he went all the way with a rush.

In the cold hours long after midnight he was on the ground tending the fire when he heard a soft sound beyond the limits of the light. He unslung the rifle and felt the thumping of his heart.

It's there. It's watching you.

He turned toward the tree. He heard the crush of dry pine needles. He cocked the gun and backed toward the tree, feeling behind him for the rope. Something moved on the edge of firelight. An enormous, shadowy form emerged from blackness. It rocked from side to side. A hoarse roar enveloped Baylor.

He fired the right barrel, and then the left. The thing came in, bellowing. Straight across the fire it charged, scattering embers. Baylor had another cartridge out, but he dropped it and clubbed the rifle. He was completely stripped now of all the thinking of evolved and civilized man.

The bellowing became a strangled grunt. The thing was down, its hind legs in the flames. It tried to crawl toward Baylor, and then it was still. Baylor rammed another cartridge in and fired a third shot. The great hulk took the fearful impact without stirring.

Cordite rankness was in Baylor's nostrils as he kicked embers back toward the fire and put on fuel with shaking hands. The stench of burning hair sickened him. He pulled the flames away from the hind legs of the beast.

He had known what he was up against from the moment the animal had stood higher than a horse there on the edge of firelight, then dropped to the ground to charge. He had killed a grizzly bear.

When the flames were high, he examined it. The feet were huge, misshapen, lacking the divisions of pads. All four were tortured, scrambled flesh that had fused grotesquely after being cruelly burned. Along the back and on one side of the bear were scabby patches where the hair had come back crisp and short. Around the mouth the flesh was lumpy, hideous from scar tissue. The jaws had been seared so terribly that the fangs and front teeth had dropped out. He lifted one of the forelegs with both hands. There were traces of claws, some ingrown, the others brittle, undeveloped fragments.

The forest fire several years before! The bear had been a cub then, or perhaps half grown. The poor devil had been caught by the flames, probably against the rocks, since only one side was scarred. He pictured it whimpering as it covered its face with its forepaws. And then, when it could no longer stand the pain and fear, it must have gone loping wildly across the burning forest mat.

Before it recovered it must have been a skinny, tortured brute. No wonder it had gone crazy afterward at the smell and sight of flames.

He found one of his bullet holes in the throat. That had to be the first shot, when the grizzly had been erect. The other must be in the shoulder that was underneath, and it would take a horse and rope to make sure. He cut into a lump on the shoulder that was up. Just a few inches below the tough hide, under the fat, he found a .45 bullet. One of Bill Paxton's, probably.

That was enough examination. The poor, damned thing.

He was asleep by a dead fire when the savage crackling of gunfire roused him shortly after dawn. He sat up quickly. The firing ran furiously, somewhere near the West Wall. Then the sounds dwindled to single cracks, at intervals. A little later Big Ghost was quiet.

Baylor hoped there was truth in what Owen had said about the basin going back to range. For the first time in days he heard the wakening sounds of birds. Before he had been listening for something else.

He was asleep in the sun out in the park when the clatter roused him. The ranchers were coming. Kullhem, his left arm in a sling, was riding with Baldray in the lead. Farther back, a man was tarpaulin-draped across his saddle.

Owen and Paxton spurred ahead to Baylor, who pointed toward the tarpaulin.

"Orahood," Owen said. "The only man we lost."

Baylor was stabbed by the thought of Orahood's wife alone at Sky Hook, with a baby coming on.

Paxton said: "We caught 'em foul on Windy Trail! We broke their backs!"

"Oregon?" Baylor asked.

"He tried one of his little tricks."

Owen kept looking toward the forest.

"It's there," Baylor said wearily.

Men gathered around the grizzly.

"Good Lord!" Crosby kept saying. "Would you look at the size of that!"

"That must have been a spot of fun, eh, Baylor?" Baldray frowned, not satisfied with his words. "You know I mean a narrow place . . . a tight one."

Raven was all around the bear, like a fly. "How did he get food while he was recovering from those burns?"

"He healed himself in a swamp," Kullhem growled. "There's always cows and calves bogged down in the swamps."

"A remarkable specimen, nonetheless." Raven drew a sheath knife. "I'll have a look at that stomach and a few other organs." He hesitated. "Your bear, of course, Baylor. You don't mind?"

"Yeah." Baylor shook his head slowly. "Leave him be, Raven. The poor devil suffered enough when he was alive."

Raven stood up reluctantly. He put his knife away. "I guess I understand."

Baldray's bony face showed that he understood. "Fire killer," he said. "The poor damned beast."